Aliens Crashed in My Back Yard

A Kind of a Love Story

by Songstress Selena M
as told to **Mike Van Horn**
with lyrics from her hit songs

Book 1 of the **Agate and Breadbox** trilogy

Copyright 2020 Mike Van Horn, all text, lyrics, and illustrations.
Published by Galaxy Tall Tales, **galaxytalltales.com**
an imprint of The Business Group Publications.
San Rafael, California
ISBN 978-0-9714114-0-1

Cover and illustrations
VShane www.vshane-art.com

Book Design
William M. Van Horn
inmystudio@hotmail.com

What Readers Are Saying

"A wonderful story. I am not much of a fan of contemporary science fiction, but I like the way you write. You have revived my adolescent fascination with science fiction." Thomas Heaven

"This story doesn't fit the typical sci fi mold of far future, evil aliens, dystopian Earth. It's a story of self-discovery, with an alien and some advanced technology."

"Your writing has the voice of a good storyteller sitting with friends reminiscing about events in real life." Terry Lynn Tuttle

"Great story! Kept me coming back to find out what was going to happen next. A good mixture of science, action, and philosophizing. It reminds me a bit of Asimov's writing--maybe because the voice is straightforward, without poetic flourishes. I'm looking forward to the next book." William, Arkansas.

"Too much sci fi focuses on hard-to-imagine technology. But nothing in your stories requires a high understanding of technology or astronomy. "And the lyrics are great—girl with an attitude." Justin Boote, Barcelona

"I love the narrative voice – down-to-earth (no pun intended), strong, and funny. And how could I pass by the title?" Sue Weems

"I love the parts where the alien sings along with the narrator. Very touching." Ann, Paris.

"Your characters' personalities and voices are strong and clear, even the little alien who doesn't say a word in English. I connect with the alien, Breadbox. Her singing, her tone, her innocent questions and guilt. I find myself thinking it does not matter what she looks like." MC D'Alton, Australia.

"I love your story, your characters, the narrative, the tone, and the whole kit-and-kaboodle. What an enjoyable read. What a commanding writer you are." Trula, Arizona.

"You have a wonderful way with words and tell a great story. With your insight I might just think you've had some meetings with 'special Aliens.'" Milton, San Diego.

Table of Contents

Epilogue - A Glimpse Forward

Extras for My Readers

Song Lyrics

Mike Van Horn

Want to Read More?

Dedicated with love to my wife B.J.,
fellow traveler through life
and cosmic tall tales

Gratitude to my two critique groups, other writers who—annoyingly—don't think every word I write is perfect, but who have greatly improved my prose: The 4-F Society and Becoming Writer.

Also to copy editor Rosina Wilson, who reined in my more fanciful flights of weird language and brought about needed consistency.

To Karen Gault Skelly who transcribed many of my weird chapters after I tromped around the hills dictating them on my iPhone.

To Kyle Kosup who did my author website and helped me get this published.

To Troy Lush, who composed the music for my lyrics; to singer Mari Mack who became the voice of Selena; and to Christopher Krotky, who produced them.

And finally to graphic designer Shane Colclough who produced beautiful covers and turned my scribbles into likenesses of my characters.

1. California Woman Risks Fate of Entire Human Race

"Secrets of Immortality Gleaned from Alien Remains," trumpeted The New York Times on page 1, sounding like the tabloids.

Yeah, those were the aliens they dug up from my property up along the California coast near Bodega Bay. And yes, I admit it, I was the one who had buried them, with the help of my friends. Had to. They were dead, and we didn't have enough freezer space to hold them.

Also, we wanted to honor them, and NOT let the government cut them up to learn their secrets. But they did that anyway. And they took the spaceship from me.

Yet there was another who survived, and it's her story I want to share with you.

My fans have been clamoring for the real story. I'm Selena M—named "Songstress of the Year" by Time Magazine not that long ago. Even if you're not familiar with my music, you've no doubt seen my name in the tabloids lately. "She's a ditzy chick, and in way over her head!" just for starters. There's been so much baloney issuing from the media meat grinder. I've resisted telling the whole truth because it doesn't make me look too good. But that's over. I want to give it to you straight, right from the beginning.

Selena means "of the moon." But despite what some media rags say, I never claimed to be a moon maiden. I'm French, or at least French Californian. You sometimes see my name as Berthe, which alas is what my parents named me.

My name for the alien who survived was Breadbox—which she never really understood, even though we had spent the long days of her convalescence learning each other's language and stories.

She was such an odd-shaped entity, kind of like a cross between a squid and a centipede with a head shaped like a parking meter sticking out the top, and an ever-changing number of pseudopods instead of feet and fingers. And a band of metal around her middle. I told Sheriff Jim that she was bigger than a breadbox, and the name stuck. "Bigger than a breadbox" is a throwback to my Gran's time, from a show called Twenty Questions, where everything in the world is either bigger or smaller than a breadbox.

Her name for me was Agate. She called me her gem of agate among all the infinitesimal grains of sand on the unnamed beaches of the cosmos. I was moved to tears, because I see myself as no more than an insignificant bit on the cosmic shore.

I am so sorry that she was not able to return to her own people and home world. And I miss her more than I can say.

But let's go back to the beginning.

*   *   *

Clay and me and the Osbornes were sitting on my deck watching the sun set out over the Pacific Ocean—magnificent, brilliant oranges, lavenders and greens. My neighbor Meg Osborne—Sheriff Jim's wife—was expounding on the green flash, when there was, indeed, a large flash behind the fogbank, low over the horizon. What could it be? Lightning? A missile test? As an inveterate weather watcher, I automatically started counting seconds until the thunder arrived. I got up to sixty before I gave up, figuring that little sound would travel more than twelve miles.

Perhaps another minute later came the distant spreading boom, rolling at us across the surface, echoing off the hills behind, then off the higher cloud layers. It was a very large boom of some sort. And then, whistling over us, something hit the old cypress tree with a thwack, strong enough to knock the dead limb off, which fell directly onto my artichoke patch. I was up like a shot, and ran back there, almost jumping over the fence in my haste.

"What the heck flew here?" I wondered aloud, as I looked back toward the sea. "Was it related to the off-shore explosion we just heard?" I gingerly lifted the dead limb from my artichoke plants to survey the damage, and to find the cause—and there it was. As I lifted the limb, the culprit unwound and fell off onto the ground. I saw a little chain with an amulet of some piece of dull metal on it. The chain was very fine and woven. I picked it up, then dropped it. Wow, hot! I got a stick and picked up the chain, and noticed it was quite heavy, like a piece of lead—or even heavier. Uranium? Yikes! Maybe it's radioactive! I dropped it. My friends were gawking timidly as if they were watching the bomb squad at work.

"Clay!" I called out. "Do you still have the radiation meter? You know, the one we used to see if we had any radon leaking in my crawlspace?"

"You are one crazy woman," he responded. "You should leave that thing alone." But he did what I requested, as usual. Clay knows where everything is at my house, even though he can't find anything in his own place. He produced the meter right away, and we held the sampler by this amulet. No reading. Batteries dead? We gave it a test, and it looked like everything was working well. It read the background radiation okay. But no reading from this. Apparently it's not radioactive. But it's sure heavy.

"Heavier than a lead sinker of that size, I'd say," said Clay thoughtfully, as he rolled it in his fingers.

"I thought lead sinkers were illegal," said Meg.

"Well, I've got a lifetime supply, and the hell with the fish. I can't catch 'em anyway."

I touched it. The cylinder was cooling down, still warm. I picked it up. It was a stubby cylinder, maybe a half an inch in diameter and an inch long. In the fading dusk light it appeared to be a plain, indistinguishable gray. We took it inside, shined the Maglite on it. The plain gray transformed into subtle colors, like a pigeon's wing in bright sunlight.

"What is this thing?" asked Jim Osborne. He's a Sonoma County deputy sheriff. "Was there an aircraft that crashed or exploded, and this is something worn by one of the passengers?"

"Well, if someone had it around their neck the chain must have sliced their head off," opined Clay with a grimace. "But I don't see any sign of blood."

"I'm sorry, folks," said Jim, stretching, shaking off the chardonnay. "I guess I'd better mosey back to the station and get in pre-disaster mode. Something's surely gonna hit the fan tonight with this." We could already hear the radio squawking from his car in my driveway, and then his cell started chirping. "Meg, no need for me to drag you off," he said to his wife as he crunched across my gravel drive.

But that was pretty much the end of our little party.

Later that night I was lying in bed, reliving the night's events. Something bothered me. I couldn't put them out of my mind. We had listened to the radio and TV for reports of a crash at sea, and there was nothing. I called Sheriff Jim again, and he said they'd received a number of reports and presumed it was a sonic boom. Yet it still bothered me. Something was incomplete here.

That night I dreamed of lying on my lounge in the back yard as I often do, looking up at the blue sky. A fly buzzed lazily across my field of vision, a couple of feet above my eyes. Just at that moment, a small plane also flew across my field of vision—perhaps several thousand feet up. The fly appeared to be the same size, moving at the same speed as the airplane. They were two equivalent objects for a moment. I sat bolt upright in bed, instantly awake, shivering. That was it! There had been two objects, one close by that hit our tree, and another one higher, whooshing through the air.

I could scarcely wait till dawn. At first light I loaded my thermal cup with high-test coffee, climbed up on my roof, and looked east to see where a whoosh might have carried something larger and higher. Up on the hills behind my house are wild acres of scrub, a few trees, and lots of poison oak. Might be on my land, or it might be on Farmer Jed's up behind me. Whatever "it" was. Fired up the Jeep, took off up the hill, put it in low-low four-wheel drive, chugged over the rocks. Got up to the top and could see nothing, nothing at all. Got out, walked around, and looked down at my house to see where something might have gone. It might have been much higher—maybe it went clear over the ridge and on east into the redwoods. Or maybe it was my imagination.

"Whoa! There it is!" I yelled out. Oh, Lord, it was an aircraft, crashed down there in the least accessible place, clear back at the deep end of Poison Oak Gulch, up under the old oak tree. I had waged war against this poison oak ever since I'd moved up here, so that I could get back to the spring at the head of the gulch without turning into one huge rash. So I had carved out a pathway down there.

I bounded down the narrow path, avoiding the insidious bright-green leaves that were everywhere, ready to grasp me if I veered off course. One slip would plunge me into Poison Oak Hell. There it was—the tangled wreckage. What the heck was it? It was no aircraft I could remember seeing—maybe it was just a piece of one. I edged on down, around the big boulder. Oh, this was only a fragment. Look up there, another whole piece. It looks like half an airliner, but dark gray like a military plane. No sign of smoke or of life. I approached it warily.

Bigger than it looked. It had skidded through several hundred feet of poison oak and chaparral. I saw a huge tear in the side. I looked in. Dark. No windows. Smelled very funky. I had my flashlight, but naturally it was way back up at the Jeep. Stuck my head in, breathing through my mouth on the theory that if I couldn't smell it, it wouldn't hurt me. My eyes got used to the gloom. It was cool and dim within. It looked more like a space shuttle. Were there bodies?

Something was alive here! There was a tiny cry, a whimper, like a baby raccoon makes after it's been chastised by its mother. A movement and a sigh. I edged closer. There, hanging from the ceiling, was somebody, something. No, things were upside down, so a live being was hanging from the floor, in some harness. Not a person. It looked more like an octopus or a squid, but a stubby one. It was shivering and sighing. I bolted out through the opening, ran back to my Jeep. The hell with the poison oak—got to get that flashlight.

I was back in no time with the big heavy-duty flashlight that had seen me through many storm crises. With it I lit up the interior of this thing, and there before me was a tableau out of this world. I mean literally. It was a live being, but not a human being. Nor animal. It sure wasn't an escapee from any Earth zoo. I had stumbled into a crashed flying saucer, apparently. This being looked to be in bad shape. It was amazing it wasn't dead, but it looked badly injured. A puddle of blood or other bodily fluids grew beneath it.

It saw me, too, with two big eyes opening and closing on the ends of quivering stalks. What did it think of me? That I was there to do it in? What should I think of it? Was it going to attack me the first chance it got? Huh! Hanging there upside down like a truncated octopus, it didn't look particularly threatening.

It took me a minute to sort out what was live being and what was

4

instrument or uniform. I noted a breathing orifice at the base of what looked like a neck. Its skin was mottled gray—dark with lighter gray splotches. Skin looked loose and saggy, like a puppy about to grow. It opened an eye, looked at me. Then a second eye on a stalk. They were truly like the eyes of an octopus. The eyes regarded me. Solemnly? With terror? With malevolence? How the hell would I know?

When I think back on this event, what I did was incredibly foolhardy. Outside of this thing's conscious intentions, who knows what kind of disease I could have caught from it. Or unleashed on humanity. But I didn't even think of all that. Here I was, in the presence of a being not from Earth, which had arrived via some kind of vessel, apparently a spaceship. It was hurt; it needed my help.

Besides, I was looking for the next thing in life. I was tired of my same ole, same ole; I had all the money I needed; my so-called music career was fine, but it wasn't an all-consuming passion. If you must know, I was feeling bored with it. I needed something new in my life. What better to do than to get involved with an injured alien bug-eyed monster?

So there I was, going through every cliché of old science fiction movies—gesturing friendship, "I'm a friend, peace, I mean you no harm." Since it probably didn't speak English, I spoke slowly and loudly, as if it were a foreigner. I waved and pointed. But what do gestures mean? I might as well have flipped it the finger. It twittered in response, an incredibly sad song, a bit like a mourning dove. The sound broke my heart.

I did have the presence of mind to look around, to see if it had any Godzilla-type allies. But no. This compartment was quite small. There was one other similar chair or harness, but the other apparatus was empty.

I went over to this being and tried to communicate through gestures that I would be willing to help it down and out of the harness and put it on the floor, or whatever was beneath my feet here. I gestured, kind of removing straps and harnesses and lowering it gently downward. It responded by repeating "Ooww, oooww, oooww." Did that mean yes, please; don't touch me, you brute; or I'm hungry and you look really tasty?

Being a softhearted idiot, I went for the first option. I described through gestures what I was going to do, one move at a time, and then I did it. The strap release was not difficult at all. I figured I'd probably release the straps and whatever the thing was would fall to the floor and kill itself. So I stood beneath it to brace the fall, then carefully loosened one clasp at a time. It watched what I was doing, and pointed out with one of its little finger-like pseudopods which strap to do next.

When I had finally released it from all the straps, the alien fell on me. It was as heavy as a dead pony. The poor creature looked up at me, raised two pseudopods, two stubby tentacles, waved them in an intricate pattern, and crooned in a way that looked just like the pattern it was signing—if you can understand that. It was lying there, and gestured to me then to turn it right side up, I guess—and put its pseudopods down. Which I did.

5

More crooning and waving.

Then the alien pointed, made some more sounds, and a little corkscrew motion with the end of its tentacle or whatever—which now looked more like a long finger. I went over to what it was pointing at, and there was a compartment to open. By twisting the latch in the way the creature had indicated with its corkscrew motion, the storage compartment opened. I could see that it was full of supplies.

The alien said words to me, which naturally I could not understand. But they were recognizable as words, not moans or croons. I looked at it blankly. It picked up instantly that I didn't understand, and reverted to croons and gestures. English and French, baby, that is all I understand—I'm weak on Martian.

It gestured for me to haul things over to it, so I brought stuff out of this compartment. It pointed to a particular thing; I held it up; it looked like some sort of first-aid pad. The being and I together spread this over this huge gash in its side, which was no longer bleeding—or whatever passes for blood—but clearly looked as life-threatening a gash as one could imagine.

My alien started croaking for something else, which I couldn't understand. It was pointing back toward a part of the vessel that was greatly damaged, and making excited noises. I went back and looked. I would point to things, then look back at it. Clearly, I wasn't getting what it wanted.

The poor thing made a little "boop" sound, pointed at me, and I went back over. It was pointing at my face, tracing out a line down my face. What? I didn't get it. Then a gesture, using several tentacles. Like a hula dancer's hands. Waves. Then a downward cascade. Over and over again. Then it pointed at my face, tracing a line, almost touching me. What the . . . Sweat running down my face! Water! H2O. It was thirsty. Hanging upside down from a harness after a near-fatal crash, and it was thirsty. Where's the canteen?

I looked around. The enormity of what was happening hit me. My knees buckled. Here I was communicating with an alien being, an entity from a different planet. Maybe a different solar system (most likely). Crashed. At my mercy (hopefully).

No canteen, but I had my cell phone, right in my jacket pocket. Should I call NASA? The tabloids? The sheriff? The government? My lawyer? My publicist? Holy shit! I could be famous. Or eaten. Or else, I could be the person who brought the plague to Earth.

I looked at this poor thing huddled on the floor at my feet, whimpering for water. I could flick it the sweat off my brow. Snatches of sci-fi movies flashed through my mind. Government scientists carving up alien beings to learn the secrets of their metabolism. In the end, the aliens were always killed. They were either hostile or misunderstood.

Then there was the genre of alien abductions. People were snatched off the face of the Earth by flying saucers; weird sexual experiments took place. And then they were returned to Earth to tell an unbelieving reporter from Newsweek.

Well, this one had apparently flown in too low, and kaboom! So sexual experiments were out of the question for the time being. But what should I do? What should I do right now? If you wanted to inform the U.S. government or the United Nations that an alien had just crashed on your property, who should you call? INS? It was Sunday—they wouldn't be there anyway. So I called my buddy Clay. Got out my cell phone, called him. The beast was clearly interested in this show of technology. I got his voice mail. "Clay, if you're there, pick this damn thing up right now—I don't care what you're doing. It's me." Clay picked up his phone. "What's up?"

Clay, high school teacher

"Clay, listen carefully. Something extraordinary has happened, and I need your help."

"Are you all right?"

"Yeah, I'm fine. I don't want to go into detail over the phone. You know where Poison Oak Gulch is?"

"Yeah, I been there."

"Get your ass up here right now. Bring with you a bottle of purified water. You got that?"

"Yeah, I guess I can."

"Bring your little videocam, and make sure you bring an extra power pack and some flashlights. You know where those are?"

"Sure, in your place I do."

"Well then, bring mine. But get up here fast, and don't let anybody else know about this."

"Anybody can be listening over a cell line."

"Well, so get your ass up here. And Clay, keep your phone handy. I might think of some other things and need to call you in the next few minutes."

"Yes, ma'am. Whatever you say, boss."

"Call me if you absolutely have to, but mainly just get here. Come up the left side of the cut. You'll see my Jeep parked up at the north lip. On that side, you can get here without having to wade through all the poison oak."

"Gotcha. So what'd ya find there?"

"Just come. You'll be glad you did. "

2. Dead and Dying Aliens

I've been a sweet stuff singer
All my girlie years
Airy, frothy little ditties
Full of love and tears
From "Cotton Candy Lovin'" on Inner-Galactic Journey album
by Selena M

What do you do with three aliens who crash-land on your back hillside? Yeah, there were three. One alive; two dead—killed in the crash—their bodies bashed and smashed in their harnesses. The living one badly injured.

After Clay got there and saw what I had there in my poison oak patch, for the first five minutes all he could say was, "Holy shit. Holy shit. Holy shit!" It wasn't until he calmed down and we poked around in the rest of vessel, clambering over the strewn debris of equipment, that we found the two dead crewmembers.

The living one, whom later I called Breadbox, but right now was just the non-dead alien, we decided our top goal was to keep her alive. I figured out how to give her some water, by pouring it into a loose piece of material that was vaguely saucer shaped, and holding it up to her. (Why did I call her a "she" from the very beginning? It turned out I was right, but I had no way of knowing then.) She needed a doctor. An ambulance. We should bring in Dr. Ellmon, and maybe the coroner, what's his name.

Let me tell you what we didn't do. We didn't inform the authorities. Why not, you might ask? Aliens, biggest story in history. Advanced technology. Possible public health threat, worldwide pandemic caused by germs from across the galaxy. A smart person, a good citizen, would have called the government so they could take charge and do the right thing.

Well, it's like this. Among my friends in the city, I'm known as the hard-hearted conservative. I own a rifle. But up here, with my friends along the coast, I'm thought of as the bleeding-heart liberal. These folks, and this includes our sheriff Jim, do not trust the government at all. They all have gun racks in the back windows of their pickup trucks. To them, the purpose of guns is to protect ourselves from our own government, or from invasions by the United Nations. So when we discussed what to do, the option of calling in the Feds never even came up. We knew what would happen. We'd all seen ET and The X-Files.

So we couldn't bring in our local doctor, Old Man Ellmon (we call him "Old Man" even though he's younger than me), because he's a damn liberal, and a stickler for regulations. He'd turn us in. Instead we called in the vet, who doesn't want me to use his name. (I'll call him Doc.) He's head of the local chapter of Sons of American Freedom, but he's done great work on Clay's horses and my old dog Buddy after he tangled with a coyote—rest his soul. (Buddy, not the coyote. I tracked that varmint down and shot him, for killing a member of my family.)

Two dead aliens, one still alive, barely. So what are we going to do with them?

Let's back up a bit. After Clay got there and stopped hyperventilating, we sat in stunned silence and stared around us. It was all so . . . alien! Yet at the same time recognizable. We could look at things and kind of figure out what they were for—even though the crew of this vessel had been so different. It's as if there's a law of convergent evolution for aircraft and space vessels regardless of where they come from. They all have to be able to handle the same functions. I must say, however, that this cabin was much less cluttered than photos of the space shuttle I've seen. But equally tight and claustrophobic.

Speaking of claustrophobia, it's Clay who hates caves. To explore this vessel, which was obviously lying upside down—and totally dark—we had to crawl through a passageway that was like tight underground caves I've been in. I had to creep forward on hands and knees, holding the big flashlight in one hand, and peer around. Clay, the big, brave manly man, couldn't handle this at all. So I did it. Plus, I fit better in skinny places than Clay's six-foot-four frame.

That's when I found the two dead crewmembers. It was terrible. They looked—and smelled—like road kill. Mangled, torn bodies in the same kind of harnesses. Dripping the juices of their former lives. I just lost it. I trembled and shrieked and upchucked last night's dinner. Clay had to crawl back there with me, despite his fear.

Wow! How do we tell the remaining one that her comrades are dead? She's marooned all alone on an alien world.

She kept looking and pointing toward the rear, where her fellow crewmembers had been. We had to let her know: I crawled back there, and brought out artifacts from each.

The tough work always comes down to the woman, right? I communicated the best I could. At last she got it. I could tell by her reaction—she trembled and twitched and shuddered. A tiny mewling sound. Seemed like crying to me. So I joined her, broke down and bawled. I held her, as best I could. Like trying to hug a twitchy microwave oven.

Clay was so embarrassed to see me crying. I was embarrassed, too. "Don't you dare tell," I growled. "I'll rip your heart out!"

Clay fumbled for his handkerchief, handed it to me, and mumbled, "If we're going to do anything, we've got to bring in Doc." Clay called him by cell. I let him explain the whole dang situation. It took Doc a long time to get past thinking it was a big joke. Finally, Clay convinced him to take it seriously, keep his mouth shut, and come help us. "Better bring a couple of body bags." After a second, he added, "Maybe three."

When Doc got there, with his bag of magic tricks for big animals like horses, he started checking her over with no hesitation.

What amazed me about Doc, knowing how worked up he can get about people with certain political opinions, is how matter-of-fact he was. He may have his problems with human foibles, but he is truly a healer of animals. Doc saw this poor alien as a beastie in need, so he went into full vet mode.

Doc, veterinarian and survivalist

We then had the conversation about what to do next. Clay and Doc and me. I did not want her to be carried away by men in white coats.

Doc said, "Maybe we should put it out of its misery. Looks close to death. I've had to put down many animals."

"No way!" I pleaded. "Let me nurse her back to health!"

"Bad idea!" Doc shot back. "You can't do this by yourself! Even if it doesn't die."

"So help me out."

Doc grimaced and huffed, but relented: "Okay, but if this one dies, we're calling in help."

"Should we tell Sheriff Jim?" asked Clay.

Doc scoffed. "How would we keep it a secret from him?"

"I'll do the deed." I called Jim on my cell, but could only leave a message.

We had to somehow retrieve the dead crewmembers. Couldn't leave them there.

We managed to get the two dead ones into the body bags and drag them out through the narrow, dark passageway, past the survivor and out the gash in the hull.

What to do with two dead aliens? We'd have to freeze them or bury them. Nobody had the freezer space, so we buried them, right near their craft. No caskets, but in the body bags from Doc.

Clay dug two small graves, using the spade I keep in the back of my Jeep. Thank goodness the soil is deep and soft here along the creek. But still, he dug only a couple of feet deep. We held an impromptu funeral, with a combo of fundamentalist and atheist platitudes. Doc was thankfully forgiving of my cynical secular philosophy.

Later, I put flowers on their graves, and made grave markers with a couple of extra flagstones from behind my shed. I used a permanent marker, but I didn't know what to say, least of all their names, so I just wrote down the date of the crash.

We stood there in the afternoon sun, reflecting on this amazing event. Clay asked the thing we were all wondering about: "Where did they come from?"

Doc's brow furrowed, "Don't think they came from the Moon. Mars, maybe."

Clay shook his head. "Naw, we got our rovers crawling all over Mars, and they've never found anything like this."

"Maybe they've been in hiding, waiting for us to show up so they can follow us home." That seemed too preposterous even for Doc. "How do we know they're not from somewhere on Earth? The Chinese or Russkies, cooked up in some lab. Or the North Koreans." For Doc, every cloud has a silver conspiracy lining.

"Must be one of the other planets," mused Clay vaguely.

I shook my head. "Nothing like this ship came from Jupiter or Uranus or Saturn. They're just big frozen gas balls. You've seen the documentaries."

Even with our level of cosmic ignorance, we saw that if they didn't originate from any other planet in our solar system, they had to have come from somewhere else. We knew all the possibilities from seeing various sci-fi flicks over the years. This would be a voyage of many lifetimes. Had they traveled in suspended animation? Maybe they were like androids—machines that were in essence immortal. No, those broken bodies were definitely flesh and blood, or something quite similar.

Did they have some kind of warp speed? Clay, who is a high school teacher, pointed out repeatedly that this violated the universal laws of physics. But I wasn't so sure. When you're confronted with undeniable facts that contradict your theories, what gives?

Doc confessed that this whole thing troubled him because he couldn't reconcile it with Bible teachings. These beings couldn't be made in the image of God. But the same shift in perception was happening with him. You could see his wheels grinding—flesh and blood facts confronting deeply held beliefs.

Our remaining alien was shaking and trembling and drawing into a fetal position. Seemed to be shriveling. "She's not long for this world," I said softly, shaking my head. I gave her more water. What else could we do for her? Alas, not much.

Doc's phone blurted out the beginning of Stars and Stripes Forever. "Gotta take this. Yeah, what's up?" Frown, then, "I better go. Three goats got into some bad garbage. Belly aches. And that's something for a goat. Communal farm up on the ridge, those damn hippies. I'll bring some more stuff when I come back."

"I'm sticking here with you," Clay said protectively.

"I know you've got choir practice this evening, Clay. I'll be all right here." He protested, but I knew he had to go; he's the choir director. I pushed him outside. "She probably won't last out the night. I'm staying here with her so she doesn't die utterly alone."

"I'll be back afterward." Then he added over his shoulder as he headed out, "It's an it, not a she. Better not personalize it. Just a dying alien being. Don't let yourself get attached." Easy for a man to say.

I hurried back to my house and gathered up a few essentials. I hadn't had anything to eat all day, so I made myself a humongous sandwich, and gulped it down with a beer. Not very ladylike, I know. But on my concert tours, hopping from city to city, sandwich gulping is what keeps me going.

What else would I need overnight? I brought back my down sleeping bag and an inflatable pad—my joints aren't as limber as they used to be.

By the time I got back it was dusk, hardly twenty-four hours since the crash. I looked in. She hadn't moved. I spread out my bag and curled up near her as the last light faded away.

Doc and Clay both got delayed, and ended up not returning, but they did check in by phone. You don't suppose these two strong men were afraid of the dark, with alien ghosts rising from the ground?

Then Sheriff Jim called back. I dreaded his call. Even though he's a good friend, I always get a bit nervous when I'm being questioned by The Law. Part of me assumes I'm guilty of dastardly crimes. Especially when he started out in his "Just the facts, Ma'am" voice. It was during this conversation that I first referred to my visitor as "Breadbox." Sheriff's deputies on this coastline get to see a lot of weird stuff, so hearing about an alien in a flying saucer didn't faze him as much as I expected.

I lay there in the dark talking to her. I asked her questions. Where are you from? Why did you come here? What happened? What was your life like? How old are you? I got no response, of course. Wasn't sure she was still alive.

I told her my entire life story. I confessed many things that I'd never revealed to anyone else. Including myself.

How I was strong and self-assured on the outside, but inside? Not so much. How I'd come to the road less traveled, but had stayed on the freeway.

How I had dumped the only guy I'd ever truly loved because of my stupid music career, and all my tours. How I often studied myself in the mirror, standing sideways, wondering if I should bother trying to keep myself slim and in shape, or whether I should let it all go and enjoy my cheeseburgers. How I knew I could never go for Clay, even though I knew he had a big crush on me, and he'd be a damn good catch for an aging chick like me.

How I'd never even tried to publish the songs that were the most important to me because I didn't think they were marketable, and instead churned out all these maudlin ballads. Which of course made me a shitload of money, and allowed me to buy my dream property here on the coast, psychically as far as possible from La La Land. But which left me with this empty hole here near the core of my being.

I began to hum this one melody I'd written years before, and had never performed in public. It was my internal anthem—the music for my secret self.

My alien companion, lying in the dark covered by a horse blanket, in a tiny, squeaky voice, hummed along with me.

3. Nursemaid to an Ailing Alien

If the world only knew me
And knew what I could do
If the world could only see me
And appreciate the view
And no scoffing, "She's just a girl."
From "Anthem to My Secret Self" on Inner-Galactic Journey album

Day 2. Over-the-hill rock star and gravely injured alien interloper on life support.

I was up at the crack of dawn, to see my guest looking intently at me with her large octopus eyes. She had survived the night, surprise surprise. She looked alert, yet inert. Just lying there, kind of deflated looking, but her eyes on the eyestalks were wide open and looking all over. What did she most need? For me in the morning, it's take a pee, get some coffee, and avoid looking in the mirror.

She chirped and squeaked a little ditty, waving two tentacles in harmony with her speech. One tentacle in a little corkscrew, then straightened it out, pointing it at something. Against one side was a gadget that looked like a coiled hose with a complicated valve on the end. She wanted that. I pulled it over. She pointed to a place in the metal band around her midriff, and I surmised she wanted me to plug this thing in there. I could hear a slight sound from the device, like it was beginning to operate. Amazing to me that there were systems on this vessel that were still able to function after its horrific crash. And it was upside down. You'd think, how could it work upside down. But as I thought about it, it struck me that space vessels operate mostly in zero-gravity situations. Up and down are not constants. So things did work somewhat.

Presumably this was breakfast. Automatically dispensed food. After I plugged it into her side, she got visibly "reflated" in a short time. Her skin lost some of that saggy-puppydog look.

Even before the sun came up over the east ridge, I heard my compatriots returning. Clay's unmistakable old Dodge pickup, and a second one. Deep, throaty, powerful sound. Could only be Sheriff Jim's gargantuan pickup. Yep, there was wife Meg's piercing voice. "Here's her

Jeep. She must have stayed here all night!" Then a third I couldn't identify. Doc's van?

They all tromped down past the poison oak and piled in through the gap in the side of the vessel, trying to get in simultaneously, all flashlights and clumping boots. They spotted me and my "patient," and all started talking at once.

Sheriff Jim spoke loudest, voicing his concerns. "I'm really nervous about concealing this vessel, and these aliens. I don't know if we can avoid calling in the authorities on this. We can't have something like this here, on my watch."

"Jim, you are our authority here," asserted Clay. "So we've got that covered. And if I'm not mistaken, if something from outer space falls on

Sheriff Jim with wife Meg

16

your property—unless it belongs to some government—it belongs to the property owner. So this whole thing is rightfully Selena's."

Jim was puffing up his chest to rebut this claim, but the others kind of shushed him down, and he stood there fidgeting and humphing, caught between close friends and more distant professional demands.

Meg is the most excitable one, but she'd apparently been clued in by hubby Jim—Mr. Laconic. I think she viewed our visitor more as a wounded wild animal.

"Why don't you have it restrained?" she asked.

Looking at the poor thing, I saw it trembling and vibrating its tentacles. Trying to move away from us. "She's terrified!" I cried. "We're worried about what it might do to us, but we've got it outnumbered."

Doc said, "C'mon, help me carry stuff down." Jim and Clay went up to his van with him, and Meg started tidying things up, which were of course in an impossible jumble. She stacked debris into piles, so we were less likely to trip over or kick it. The guys lugged a van load of stuff back down. They rolled a gurney down the bumpy path, the kind that they use to rescue people who've been in an accident. They haul them off to the ambulance—or hearse. Along with it was an IV set, and a bunch of blankets. Then on a second trip, they brought down a propane heater. The third trip, they wheeled down a diesel generator.

Everyone bustled around, helping set things up so that Breadbox could be comfortable. Just like practiced paramedics, we lifted Breadbox up onto the gurney.

Doc was really getting into this. We'd soon have a makeshift ICU set up here under my big oak tree.

Meg had been asking nervously if this was wise. "Shouldn't we get her to a hospital? Even if it's just Doc's veterinary hospital?"

I pointed out the tube connecting her to her vessel. "I think she needs to be connected to this, for now. Don't see how we could transport this. Do you?"

"Maybe the whole thing could be moved," said Meg.

"They'd screw it up," Doc cut in. "They'd be more interested in other things than saving her. To them, she's as valuable dead as alive."

"So who's 'they'"? asked Jim.

Doc looked him right in the eye. "We all dang well know who 'they' are, now don't we, Jim?"

(In these parts, "they" refers to "heartless, intrusive, pushy government authorities.")

"You're all the government we need," Doc added.

Clay jumped in. "This means a lot to Selena. If we bring in government experts, she'll get pushed aside. For right now, we've got to do what we can. Later, after things get stabilized, that's the time to bring in others."

"So are we now going to devote our lives to caring for this creature?" asked Meg. "I, for one, can't do that."

Silence. Then me. "I can be the point person on this. After all, it happened on my property."

"I'm on board," proclaimed Doc.

"Quite an interesting veterinary challenge, eh?" said Clay. "Don't you want to bring in a real doc?"

Doc glowered at him. "Just kidding, Doc," added Clay quickly. "Why would a medical doctor be any better than you?"

Doc nodded, tight-lipped. "You mean those doctors who can only treat a single species? I'm used to looking at cross-species challenges. This just makes me expand my vision a bit more."

"What say you, Jim?" asked Clay.

Jim shook his head in resignation and said, "Well, I won't say anything for now. Let's give it twenty-four hours, then we'll see."

Twenty-four hours turned into two days, then a week, then a month and more, and Jim never did rat us out. We developed elaborate tales of how we'd cover for him if we were found out.

This didn't immediately become clear to me, but later I told my co-conspirators: "Here's what I want to do. I want to nurse her... it... back to health, help her repair her vessel, so she can get back home, and take her crew's remains." Seemed like an impossible task. Why the hell was I wanting to take this on? Hmmm. Well, why do we do anything?

That morning, after the others left, I pretty much decided to stick around and see what I could do to help our poor alien. I went back to my house to see if the rest of the world needed me for anything. It didn't. I had a momentary panic that I had not a single inquiry about my songstress services. From fame to notoriety to being ignored. It happens so fast!

But the panic quickly shifted to relief and gratitude. I took several more trips and kept bringing more stuff up. I began to wonder whether I was going to move in there or not. I saw that I was going to have to dig a latrine for myself, so I brought a shovel back down.

One last trip, I brought my guitar. My old Gibson. I call it Gibb, and it's a "he." I sat, strummed and played. Breadbox loved this and sang along in a little trilly, twittery voice. It seems like music is the universal—make that interstellar—language.

Wow! When she sang, her skin changed color! The light-gray spots began to take on a rosy hue. My featureless gray alien became a polka dot pink alien.

Let's try doing some words with each other, I thought. Sign language, pointing, speaking slowly. Breadbox squeaked and pipped back at me. Were these words? Probably, but I didn't get any connection to what I was saying.

After doing this for a while, I got a call on my cell, asking me to do a gig at the state college near Santa Rosa. Aha! So I hadn't been totally forgotten. They'd just had a performer cancel. Nice venue, decent money, normally I'd jump at it. But I heard myself say no. What does this signify?

Am I going to be a full-time babysitter here? Is this my next thing in life? Am I really abandoning my singing career?

I could see the newsflash. "Former pop star Selena M sinks from view—who knows where? Will anybody miss her?" That would never appear in the news, because nobody would miss me.

4. Sing Language

Inside I'm a hero
I often save the world
I smite the bad guys, save the good
Pretty good for just a girl!
Thank you, Super Girl!
    From "Anthem to My Secret Self" on Inner-Galactic Journey album

Day 3. Language is a slog. So little in common! What actually worked? Singing. And pointing. I tried tapping out numbers, feeling like the famous counting horse on stage. I pulled the gurney to the vessel's opening, so I could point out trees, sky and rocks. Yeah, so what?

She responded best to rousing melodies. I sang and played Gibb— everything I could think of. Quickly worked through my own published repertoire, then pieces I'd been working on. But what did she like best? Nursery rhymes and Christmas carols! Rousing tunes with a wide vocal range. She didn't much respond to "Mary Had a Little Lamb" or "Silent Night," but she jiggled and thrummed to "Pop Goes the Weasel" and "Joy to the World." And she responded to "Star-Spangled Banner" with an elaborate display of tentacles waving and vibrating and thrumming. I thought she'd stand up and salute! I wish I could have done it in full Jimi Hendrix mode.

She tried to sing back to me. It did not start out auspiciously. She squeaked and gasped and wheezed. I was afraid she was overdoing it.

Breadbox wanted something, but I couldn't figure out what it was. It was like my damn fool cat meowing! I'd go all around my house, trying everything I could think of that it might want. Out. In. Out again. Offer it food, water. Then ignore it.

But I couldn't just ignore this poor beastie! I pushed the gurney around as far as the tether would allow. I picked up all kinds of stuff from the floor, held it out to her. I opened up the little compartments nearby, pulled stuff out or pointed in.

It looked like this particular tentacle shake meant, "That's not it." Like a baby whose first word is "no." God, maybe she wants her porta potty! How long can she hold it in? I finally asked this question the only way I could think of. I pulled down my jeans and peed in the dirt just outside the opening, where she could watch. Then I pointed. Was this it? It reminded me of trying to housebreak Buddy when he was a pup.

Breadbox was fascinated by this display but showed no inclination that I was on the right track. What would she do to communicate this, anyway? Maybe cross her tentacles and hop up and down? Yet I wondered how my poor visitor was handling this particular need.

I started hauling things out from deeper in the vessel, but nothing I retrieved was what she was looking for. She pantomimed to me that she wanted to be disconnected from the life support. Despite my misgivings, I did this. I lowered the gurney as low as it could go, so she could crawl off. That did not go well. She was quite weak. She whimpered and I helped her clamber back up and reconnect her life support.

I went back and rummaged in the section where the dead crewmembers had been. Not easy to do. It was dark, and I had to crawl back there, holding on to my flashlight with one hand, walking around at a crouch and poking around for things that might be what she was looking for. Several trips bringing things back out, for which she signaled, "Nope, that's not it."

When I finally found it, I knew immediately! It was a cylinder. Over a foot long. Maybe two inches in diameter. Gray metallic look, with the same patterns as the amulet I had found initially. Very heavy. It didn't look like a weapon, though.

When I hauled the cylinder back up through the narrow tunnel, Breadbox showed visible excitement. This was obviously what she'd been looking for. She spoke to it and it trilled back to her. So, still functional! I handed it to her and she caressed it, held it in several tentacles like it was her baby.

She crooned to the cylinder, accompanied by waving her tentacles in a pattern that mimicked—or was part of—her singing.

The cylinder made noises in response—tones and chords and clicks and chattering sounds. Wow, so these two talked to each other?

It seemed like Breadbox's body WAS a musical instrument. High-pitched trills and hoots and thrums reverberated inside her. She had so many voices. On some melodies she sounded like a theremin, others a bagpipe or squeezebox.

The patches on her skin rippled different colors in time with her music, shifting from pale pink to deep mauve, against a turquoise background.

She was like a whole orchestra. She could sing multiple tones at once, plus vibrations from her tentacles, humming and thrumming like a bass drone. Hints of bagpipe and sitar and didgeridoo. It was wonderful music! But not language—not to me anyway.

It dawned on me that she was trying to tell me something. She would sing this snatch of song. Then she'd hold up the cylinder gizmo and it would make a series of noises—tones, clicks, grunts, raspberries. As soon as it finished, she'd start in again with her singing, then let the cylinder "speak" to me.

So it was a dang language translator! She'd heard me (and my buddies) speak and she'd heard me sing. So maybe she thought, aha, I'll sing to this being. But I understood nothing. The sounds emitting from the cylinder sounded like language to me, like it was trying to translate her singing, but it sure wasn't translating into English.

She kept trying. More and louder vibrating, sounding like she was getting excited or frustrated. I was afraid she'd blow a gasket. She twisted her entire body and looked around with her big, googly eyes.

And there I sat, dumb and mute. I guess those two mean the same thing. I meant dumb like stooopid. No comprendo! No se nada!

She certainly didn't hide her emotions, and it seemed I could read them better than her language. It was like working around an animal; after a while, you begin to get a sense of what it is feeling. This alien was feeling frustrated!

Breadbox

Not a verbal onslaught; it was more like being beat over the head with beautiful music. But gradually, she lost steam. After a pause, she twitched and emitted this rattle and gurgle, then fell silent, except for one bell-like tone—close to G above middle C—that emerged from a completely different orifice on her throat. Then silence. She shut down, kind of sinking onto the gurney. Her skin paled. The cylinder quacked perfunctorily and also fell silent.

What now? I felt completely inadequate, like the ignorant savage unable to comprehend the message of the advanced visitors from across the sea. What had she been trying to communicate so urgently?

Maybe "The secret of life and enlightenment and flying across the universe is yours for the asking!"

Or perhaps "The evil monsters are racing across space to invade. Alert your defenders!"

Or "I've got this terrible itch and I just can't scratch it!"

I was dumb as a stump.

Breadbox let go of the cylinder. It rolled along the gurney. I grabbed it to keep it from falling. She paid no heed, eye stalks drawn down.

I looked at it more closely. Where was its speaker—its microphone? I couldn't tell. Sheesh, was it ever heavy! Like a piece of granite—or lead.

I held it on my lap and talked to it. "Hi, my name is Selena, aka Berthe, and I sing songs for a living. What is your name?" Silence. Then it spoke. It seemed to repeat what I had said, but vowels only, no consonants. It was like trying to carry on a conversation with an accordion.

Then it tried again, inserting some pops and hisses and rasps. Next a rising chiming tone, then silence.

Hmm. Needs work on consonants. I recited the alphabet, enunciating very carefully. "Ai, bee, cee, dee, ee, eff . . ." and so on. Then I went through it again, adding words. "A, apple. B, boy. C, ceiling. D, dog . . ." all the way to "X, x-ray." Then I thought, "X, xylophone," and then a small aha! A tone! I did my best to duplicate the gizmo's rising tone. Did that mean "over to you"?

Yes! It copied my alphabet recitation. Several times. I tried to correct its pronunciation. It had trouble distinguishing b and p, and f and s. But clearly it and I were on the same task.

Numbers. Let's try numbers again. I picked up an empty beer bottle and a spoon from my growing midden in her vessel and clinked a couple of times. Let's be systematic. BINK. "One." BINK. BINK. "Two." BINK. BINK. BINK. "Three." Hmm. "Th" is a sound not in the alphabet. BINK. BINK. BINK. BINK. "Four." And so on. Then I did my up trill. "Over to you, gizmo."

It mimicked my beer bottle clink precisely, and gave a good first try on my words: "Wom. Tu. Free. For. Five. Fiks."

Needs more work on sibilants. I said, "These… three… things… writhe… with… the… weather." What an image! Sounded like a good line for a song.

The gizmo did its best to repeat that tongue twister, then went through the number sequence again.

Its counting drew our ignored visitor back to life. She chimed in, literally. "Bing... Bong, bong... Boong, boong, boong.... Bing, bong, boong, bwang!" All this emanated from the new chime orifice, not the singing hole. What should I call these openings? The talking mouth and singing mouth? She then spoke four short words from her talking mouth, and the cylinder followed with, "Wun. Tu. Fre. For." Wow, that sounded a lot like translation of actual words.

She immediately let forth a torrent of song, using both mouths, chiming, hooting, bonging, and singing bits of the melody of "Joy to the World."

I sang right back, "Joy to the world, the words will come!" This was just like in Close Encounters of the Third Kind! I was jubilant.

What have we learned here so far? She has two mouths, one on her throat for words and single sounds, and another for singing and emoting farther down on her diaphragm—along with all her tentacles and other body parts. Her skin colors ripple with the music.

She eats through a tube stuck in a hole in her side. And I have no idea how she takes a crap.

5. Morty, My Tone-Deaf Agent

Later I went back to my house for a quick food break. I nuked some leftover lasagna from last night (or had it been two nights ago?) and wrapped it in a huge lettuce leaf from my garden.

I had left my cellphone on the charger in my bedroom last trip, so only then did I discover I had some messages. Every single one was from Morty, my tone-deaf agent. A whole series, a few hours apart.

"Wassa matter? You said no to a gig!" Click Delete.

"What you got—another lover boy crisis?" Click Delete. I should be so lucky.

"You in rehab or something?" Delete. He knows I'm not into drugs. Just Malbec.

"Selena, sweetie, call me back toot sweet. I'm the guy who pays your rent, remember?"

I didn't want to talk with him. But I'd better tell him no, or he'd just keep pestering me. I was grateful when my return call went right to his voicemail.

"Sorry, Morty, no gigs just now." That was that.

No such luck. He called back within five minutes. This time I answered.

"Sel, where ya been?" His every sentence sounds like it ends in an exclamation point, even his questions. "You fall off the face of the Earth? You retired? You been in rehab? What?"

"Sorry I missed your calls."

"My job is to bring you gigs. Your job is to sing. I sell, you sing. I can't do my job if you don't take my calls, or if you turn down gigs."

"Sorry, Morty, I've been a bit preoccupied."

"Writing some new stuff?"

"Yeah, you could say that."

"Well, I got a gig where they want your oldies but goodies. It's Sonoma State again."

"I just turned them down."

"This is a different gig. They apologized—they actually apologized—for calling you on such short notice the other time. So they asked me when they could book you."

"Morty, are you short of money? Are you so hard up for commissions that you need to book me into places like this?"

25

"Listen up, Miss High Falutin'. Times aren't what they used to be. Not every gig is Madison Square Garden or the Astrodome."

He shifted from preaching to wheedling. "Come on, Selena, you've gotta go, don't let me down. I promised them. You know, if I can't rely on you, if they can't rely on me, then this whole arrangement falls apart. It really isn't about the money as much as it is just providing for people when they call, so that they'll keep calling. Or are you going into retirement?"

"No, I wouldn't say that."

"Just put together some of your standards. They're desperate."

"Oh and I'm the one they call when they're desperate?"

"No, they were thrilled when I said I thought I could get Selena M."

"Who cancelled?"

Morty, the tone-deaf agent

"One of the comeback tours. Dead Men Walking or something like that. These guys we all thought were dead a decade ago, till they came out of the shadows. Then yesterday their drummer had a heart attack."

"Well, I'm not that far over the hill yet. When is this wonderful gig?"

"About a month out. Saturday evening. Back to school night. All the incoming freshmen and their parents."

"Sounds like a really hip crowd."

Could I leave my alien for a few hours? Would I need to get a baby sitter? Who? Hey, Clay, how would you like to spend an evening alone with a funny looking alien?

I almost forgot to write the date on my calendar.

6. The Education of an Alien

Our experts tell us we share 99% of our genetic makeup with apes, 95% with pussycats and dogs, and maybe half with pond scum. Here was a being with whom I presumably shared 0% of genes—and who looked so totally different—yet we shared music and numbers and a desire to talk more to each other.

After the gig date was settled, I dashed back up to "alien central" to continue with our language lessons.

Again, we started with the numbers. I would say, "One," hold up one finger, and draw a 1 on my pad, and try to generalize. One rock. One shoe. One hand. One tentacle. I actually held up one of her arm-like tentacles. It was warmer than I expected. Then I did the same thing all over again with two.

Could the cylinder see me, as well as hear me? I saw nothing that looked like an eye or a camera, but then what did I know?

I repeated the words. The translating gizmo repeated them back to me, gradually improving its pronunciation. Then, it beepled over to Breadbox, who listened, and voila! She said a word and held up one tentacle! She said another word and held up two. The gizmo said back to me, "One. Two."

Wow! Wow! This was amazing! I whooped, "We've mastered One, Two! That's a beginning. Let's keep going. Maybe, Buckle my shoe! Three, four! Shut the door! Five, six! No alien tricks! Just kidding."

Numbers were easy for us to teach each other. We did a lot of counting, like on Sesame Street. And then pointing and naming, first concrete things like eye, feeding tube and tree, then graduating to more subtle things like sky, blue, day, night, dark, sun, stars.

That night I moved her gurney out to the opening of the vessel, so she could look up through the branches of the oak tree and see the stars. She was moved to sing a long, quavery melody, waving her upper tentacles in rhythmic patterns. It amazed me how expressive these waving patterns were. They seemed to correspond to the things she was expressing. Kind of like the hands of a hula dancer, I would say.

Verbs were tougher, but we both acted out actions, then described them. Once we got an understanding of what we were doing with each other, it went much faster. We were teaching each other our languages, of course, but we were also working out an unspoken meta-language about what we were doing here together. We had no way to say, "I am eager to learn from you," or "I'm going to demonstrate an action, then name it for you," or "I'll give you my word for it, then you give me yours." But we learned them from each other as surely as we learned "one, two, three."

Her cylinder was the intermediary. It listened, repeated back, improved its pronunciation, remembered, reminded. It was an infinitely patient teacher. Of course it knew her language, so its task was matching up the vocabulary I was teaching it with concepts and words that it and she already knew. It would translate her beeps and peeps and trills into my words when it could. It rendered her vocalizations in a voice that was closer to mine, if that makes sense.

Imagine trying to understand your pet crow, which has all kinds of vocalizations. They talk constantly, and loudly (especially just outside my bedroom window at dawn's first light). Your gizmo renders "crow speak" into English. But it also renders the crows' not-yet-translatable chatter into "squawk, rack rack," etc. until words can be assigned to it.

The gizmo was doing the same thing with Breadbox's utterances.

*   *   *

During all that time, I was smart enough to keep a written and dictated journal of everything we did and taught each other, including some video taken with my phone. If you're interested in how two such dissimilar beings can gradually teach each other their languages and more, I'll share it with you. I might even do a whole book about that. Jeez, I could probably get a PhD in "alien linguistics." (Like I need a PhD!)

So I won't go into all the detail here. But since I was spending all day every day with her, it went pretty fast. We could soon say simple things to each other without the cylinder gizmo translating.

My neighbors and co-conspirators made regular appearances, and made their own contributions to the vocabulary-building exercises. They'd bring along the most outrageous items, and take delight in naming them.

Meg brought her two ugly little dogs, which I call Snappy and Yappy. Breadbox was so excited to see them. At first I wasn't sure whether she was terrified or delighted, but it turned out to be the latter. So after that, a whole menagerie was shepherded here: cat, horse, mule, bird, goldfish in a bowl. Doc dragged a nanny goat up to the vessel and milked it in front of Breadbox, then sipped the milk. Who among us gets an education like that?

"What amazes me," I said when we were all together, "is that we are all here in this completely unique, out-of-this-world experience, and we're taking it so matter-of-factly."

"You're from California, so weirdness is bred in your bones," Clay explained. "The rest of us are from the Midwest. . ."

"Meg is from Texas," Jim put in.

". . . so we've become inured to the crazy things that happen here on the coast on a daily basis."

"With my Ozark upbringing," Doc added, "I just do what needs to be done without over-thinking it."

"I'm sure glad I have you all with me," I said.

Clay and Doc poked around in the ruined vessel to see if they could find other things useful to Breadbox. "Now we're not looking for souvenirs to take home, are we, guys?"

"No sirree, ma'am. We won't take anything that belongs to you or your pet alien," Clay chided. "But we did find something interesting, that looks unlike all the other broken debris." The guys emptied their canvas bags of an assortment of unidentifiable stuff. Included was a handful of speckled brown, oval, polished stones, like river pebbles. Each had a hole near one end, as if meant to be worn on a chain or leather thong.

"We found some pretty baubles strewn amidst the other debris."

"Wow, what could these be for?"

"Maybe art objects?"

"Musical instruments? Like castanets."

"For the bottom of her aquarium?"

"Game pieces?"

"Jewelry."

"I haven't noticed her accessorizing."

"Let's ask Breadbox."

I carried two of them over to her gurney and handed them to her. She took each in a tentacle and held them to face each other. She explained through her translating gizmo. "These we could use to communicate with each other. But we never used them because we were never separated."

Clay examined others from the stack. "They just look like polished pebbles to me. I wonder if she understood your question. How do you speak with stones? Tap them together?" he asked as he clicked two of them.

"My suspicious mind says you should hide them away," said Doc. "If somebody stumbles across your little alien stash up here, there will be some serious souvenir hunting, as you say. These are the most interesting things we've found, besides that translating device. And your aliens, of course. And the spaceship itself. Hell, if… when… somebody finds this, your hills will be crawling."

Doc was the alien's most steadfast supporter. He took her recovery on as a personal mission. I'd never seen that side of him before. I must say, Clay got a bit jealous. He kinda views me as his special friend. But since he's a high school teacher, he had to work all day, plus grade homework on weekends.

Doc was doing something right, because Breadbox gained strength. She could do okay for a while without her life-support tube. I guess it was actually more like a feeding tube. She'd climb off the gurney and scurry around on a bunch of her tentacles that became footlike. Kind of like a long-legged centipede carrying a piece of luggage on top. She ventured outside, and into the back section of the vessel, where her crew members had been found. She stayed back there a long time by herself, and I could hear her crooning softly.

Besides her centipede feet, she had tentacles left over for gesticulating and pointing and picking things up. She picked up and examined everything within reach. Breadbox kept the cylinder gizmo with her all the time, cradled against her with one tentacle spiraled around it. She carried it the way a little girl carries her favorite doll.

She was most expressive with her eyestalks and mouth. I say mouth, but she didn't use it for eating or for breathing, but only for talking and singing, as far as I could tell. Don't ask me to explain how she could use it to talk, but not for breathing.

7. Locos Only

My love is hiding in plain sight.
I keep it buried in the night.
From "High on Love" by Lucky

Clay reminded me I had agreed to sing Thursday evening at Locos Only, the local dive, in Bodega Bay. I didn't want to be pulled away from Breadbox. But Sal, the owner, had always been very good to me. I didn't want to leave him in the lurch.

"Come on, come on," coaxed Clay. "It'll be fun. You need to get out. And I want some company. You can sing there with your eyes closed. Your alien will be okay for a couple of hours. Make sure she's got some water to sip on. That keeps her going." At last he was now calling Breadbox "she," not "it."

Locos Only is down in the flats near the harbor, surrounded by boat-repair shops and run-down seafood restaurants that have the freshest fish possible. There was actually a line outside the club, people waiting to get in. My name wasn't in lights, but it was scrawled on a whiteboard by the door. I dragged Clay and Gibb, my guitar, to the front, and we edged in.

Sal played emcee and introduced me. "Tonight we are fortunate to have local star Selena M here, and she will do all requests. Let's give it up for our local favorite!" Decent applause, plus a few enthused fans. "Now, who has a request?"

Of course, "Cotton Candy Lovin'" was shouted out the loudest. My god, how many thousands of times had I sung this? Clay was right: I could sing these songs with my eyes closed. I put Gibb and my voice on automatic, and belted out several of my standards. Much of the audience was inattentive, to put it mildly. I felt like throwing the mike at this loudmouth jerk at the bar.

I finished my set. I was followed by a young chick who called herself Lucky. She had green and mauve hair, ultra-short skirt, no bra, tattoos and dangling piercings, prancing around screaming into the mike. "I sing my heart song. I give you heart on. I sing my heart song. I give you heart on." She literally spat out the "t" in heart. That was the entire lyric! Her vocal range was about half an octave, at maybe a hundred decibels. I noted that her hair was the same color as the spots on Breadbox's skin.

The audience stood up and screamed with her. She had a particular move—lifting her left knee and twisting her hips. Kind of like the hokey pokey on steroids. Or a dog peeing. Everybody in the audience was doing it along with her. Two drunk guys toppled over while trying it.

"I never sing my heart song," I muttered sullenly to Clay over the racket. "Nobody gets a 'heart on' over "Cotton Candy Lovin'" any more. Why do I bother? Come on, let's get out of here. I'm going home to care for my bug-eyed monster." I immediately regretted saying this about her. After all, she was a real singer. Clay chugged his beer and hurried to keep up with me.

We left as she was getting into her second number. "My love is hiding in plain sight. I keep it buried in the night."

That's me: hiding in plain sight. I hide on the stage in front of crowds of people.

8. A Song for Your World

Weeks passed. In my neglected house, dirty dishes and laundry and mail and dust piled up. My inbox had several thousand new emails, and there must have been at least a handful of them that I cared about. The world paid us no heed. Nobody came poking around looking for downed aircraft, let alone flying saucers. No alien invasion, for which Breadbox and crew had been the advance scouts. Nor any rescue attempt by angry extraterrestrials. I hadn't caught the intergalactic hungy-fungy from her, nor she from me. Life just kept on. Doc fussed around his "patient" doing I don't know what. I was nursemaid and tutor.

She and I were soon able to carry on simple conversations, with the gizmo as translator. I wished I could feed it a dictionary; things would have gone faster. So, what are the first things girls talk about? Why, boyfriends and sex, of course. And fashions.

Were Clay and Doc my mates, and did we have offspring? What was our status? Was I in charge? Or did they force me to stay here and care for her? Why did I wear clothing? Was my hair part of my clothing, or part of me? What was that stuff I dabbed on my face? What did I look like without my clothing? (Yeah, I'd heard that one before.) After a moment of bashfulness, I showed her. She was most fascinated by my various tufts of fur.

"How do your kind procreate?" she asked out of the blue. This was not the birds and bees talk I had imagined giving. Of course, we had to show each other how our body parts worked. She wasn't all that surprised by my equipment, since she'd studied comparative anatomy of the various civilized beings of the confederation of worlds her people belonged to. But I was astounded by hers. Here's what she told me.

Her kind have four sexes or phases of life. You could call them juvenile, female, male, and mother-in-law. She was transitioning from juvie to female. She and her crew members had been in this adolescent state of rebelliousness that happened just before they had to take a mate and raise young for a period of their lives.

"After nurturing our young, our third life phase is male."

I think my mouth dropped open at hearing this. "Are you saying that you go from being a mother raising young to being a father and fostering young?"

34

"Males father young, of course, but females care for them."

"That's often the case on this world as well," I frowned.

She kept going. "When we become male, we have to choose between being an engineer or professional, a warrior-politician, or a shaman. Mature males and females have separate life functions and may have little to do with each other."

Breadbox explained that their final stage was asexual. I called it the "mother-in-law" stage. (No offense intended to all you sexy mothers-in-law out there!) They were the conservative seniors. The oldest and most conservative of them became the Elders that made the rules everyone else had to follow. They poked their noses (or tentacles) into everybody's business, and wielded the real power. Hearing her describe them, they sounded for all the world like the cardinals in the Vatican.

Her metallic "breadbox" midriff, she was finally able to explain, was not part of her body, nor was it clothing. It was permanent—I guess more like a plate in your skull. It had to do with injuries or damage she and her people had done to themselves. But it wasn't till later that I fully understood this.

It was harder for her to explain her prior life and relationships to me, since we had nothing at hand to point to. But wait, we did in fact! I dragged out the pads of paper and markers we'd brought down here for me to write on; they'd gotten stuck in the corner behind Doc's stash. I demonstrated how to use them. Breadbox caught on instantly. She spiraled one thin tentacle delicately around the pen, and made some experimental marks. Soon she was demonstrating quite a skill for sketching.

She had two modes. With a single tentacle, she drew outlines, like a

Breadbox sketching beneath the oak tree

35

cartoonist. Then she'd pick up markers and draw with several tentacles at the same time. These were in a completely different style. You've seen illustrations where, say, a face is composed of many smaller objects, such as leaves and flowers and animals. That's the way she drew, using two or three markers simultaneously, quickly filling up the flip chart sheet with a wide variety of tiny little shapes—swirls and spirals, zigzags and stars, flowers and leaves. Only at the last moment did the subject of the drawing become apparent. Here's how she explained this.

"We are all separate and distinct beings, and I see us that way with my one mind. We are also all one, all part of the one, one spilling into the other, and I see that way with my two mind. With both, my song/dance are a part."

Yes, as she drew, she sang, and did her hula-like dance. The colors on her skin would ripple. All these synchronized. It was all part of the same communication.

Her gizmo translated her singing, but not into English, so I couldn't understand. But it was apparent she was telling a story as she drew.

With her flowing, rippling drawings, she sang soft music and did smooth, rhythmic dancing. Then she'd tear off that sheet of paper and do another with big, bold, jagged strokes and clashing colors. Then she'd switch. Her foot tentacles performed a stomping, kicking dance, and her organ-piping voice sang strident music reminiscent of Wagner.

I could see that we were going to go through many pads of paper. And markers.

Her music scales were certainly not those I was familiar with. Our musicians use different scales for different kinds of music, but, using her different voices, she would sing in two or three different scales at the same time. Her singing was strange, sometimes jarring and discordant, but hauntingly beautiful.

Oh, I could feel my mental sausage grinder taking all this in, to feed my creative song maker in the near future.

Despite her disparate scales, I noted that they fell into octaves, or what we call octaves. What is it about an octave that would carry from one world to another across the cosmos?

*   *   *

That evening she disconnected herself from her life support or feeding tube, and we went out to the edge of the oak's overhang where we could get a clear look at the riot of stars overhead. She vibrated her tentacles in excitement. She pointed at stars and sang different melodies for different stars. My guess is that our constellations looked nothing like the stars in her home sky, but she sang a whole repertoire of star songs. I did my best to capture her singing on my recorder.

When we went back into her vessel, she was still excited. She retrieved the drawing pad and began sketching different beings.

She drew herself. I could tell from the included gurney. But longer and thinner, with flowers around her head. And wings, like fairy wings, three pairs of them along her back. Drew different kinds of shapes emerging from her different mouths, perhaps representing the different sounds she makes.

She pointed at one of her sketches, which looked to me like a menagerie of strange animals, and sang a bit of melody—one of the melodies she'd sung earlier. I presumed she was describing to me the different kinds of beings that lived on different worlds. Then she circled two tentacles around the drawing of all of them and said a word that her gizmo translated as "together stars people."

"Together stars people." I really liked that.

Then her translating cylinder surprised me by giving me a whole travelogue, using its limited English, on these various beings, and what their worlds were like. It did this without any input from Breadbox, so it must have had all this canned info within it. Like a talking encyclopedia. Oh I wanted one!

"What else can your cylinder do?" I asked. "And what do you call it?" I'd been calling it the gizmo, but that lacked a certain elegance.

She spoke its name, but the cylinder had trouble finding a suitable term in English. The best it could come up with was "personal multiple function device."

"I don't know everything it can do," she confessed. "It helps us navigate the vessel, and it watches the systems, such as my feeding appliance. But many other things also. My comrade Novan, alas no longer with us, was the expert with the device."

She would hold it at tentacle-length, pointing it at some instrument on the vessel, and make a request. Like a wizard with a wand, I thought. A wand is something you wave in mysterious ways to make magic happen. Well, she didn't really wave it, but magic certainly happened. So it became a wand. A fat, sausagey wand, but a wand nevertheless. When I explained what a wand was used for, they agreed that was a good term for it, and "the wand" repeated its new name.

I quickly dubbed it "Wanda." Wanda the magic wand.

"Can your wand help you contact your people, so they can come and retrieve you?" I asked.

Her tentacles twitched with strong anxiety, which I had noted before with questions she couldn't answer.

"Do not wish to contact them," she said.

"Why not?" I was incredulous. How else would I be able to discharge my responsibility to her? "Does the wand, or the vessel, send a signal telling where you are?"

"We disabled that function. We were going to forbidden places. No communication until successful." Here she paused and twitched in the most astounding, clashing patterns. Finally, I was hearing some very interesting stories!

"If I fail, it is better that they never know."

"But surely you want to return home. And now you are recovering your health. Your vessel is destroyed, but they could come rescue you." Even as I said that, I had second thoughts about alerting an alien race of unknown temperament to come to Earth to rescue their surviving prodigal daughter and the remains of her friends. They may presume the crash was caused by hostile acts on our part. And how could I be certain that did not happen?

But she twittered negation. "They cannot come, because they do not have the instructions to get here even if I could tell them where I am."

"But your vessel knew how to get here. Surely it could tell them."

"The instructions were contained in a small metal crystal that was lost in the crash."

I immediately thought of the small amulet on a chain that had been the harbinger of her arrival when it whizzed overhead and knocked the limb off my tree. I described it to her. "Yes, that may be the crystal."

But she had no interest in sending such a signal to her home world, I could tell. Her tentacles signaled frustration and indecision and fear.

"Well, then, we'll have to get your vessel repaired, and you recovered, so that you can return on your own. Would that be a success, and not a failure?"

"If we can repair my vessel, then it should be returned to its rightful home," she said, her tentacles drooping.

She was silent for a long time, but her tentacles worked furiously. She went to the pad and drew the crash happening, and sang a clashing crashing melody along with it. Then she again went silent and calm.

"I have never been happier than relaxing here beneath the sun and stars sharing stories with you. You are my true friend." She drew a line drawing of herself and me within a circle of birds, flowers, and stars.

She hummed and trilled a little ditty I hadn't heard before. "This is a song for your world."

9. Breadbox Tells Her Story

"Together Stars People"
Title of Selena's instrumental guitar riff on Breadbox's little
ditties about different oki worlds
From Inner-Galactic Journey album

B readbox had come to the point of Choice in her life—a major life event on her world. And she had chosen wrong. She had been assigned a special role in life—the Singer of the clan's story—and she had refused it. Escaped it. Ended up here.

How'd she tell me all this? Breadbox sang and danced her stories, and Wanda the wand gave near-simultaneous translation. This made it quite difficult for me to grasp at first, but once I got the hang of it, I could follow her tales easily. Her singing pulled me right inside the story. With Breadbox, even her plain words were musical. Often a sentence would be completed by a long, pure musical tone, bell-like, or even an organ chord. Or like the chiming chord I hear when I fire up my Mac.

Numbers are best for sharing data. Words are meant for reasoning and explaining, for ideas and describing. But songs are meant for storytelling—for teaching, for sharing wisdom, for affirming community and relationships.

Here's Breadbox's story, pieced together from many days sitting under the old oak tree. I sat in my favorite lawn chair, she on the gurney Doc had brought up for her, as far out the gash in the hull of the fuselage as her life-support apparatus would allow. Often she would unplug from it and curl up on a blanket beneath the oak. I had my huge glass of sweet herbal iced tea, spiced with a bit of rum, or sometimes gin. She had her bowl of magical water concoction, dipping her short tentacle in it and dripping it over her head. Wanda was our translator, explainer and encyclopedia of all things alien. But I was gradually beginning to understand some of Breadbox's utterances directly.

Throughout her story of strange events across the cosmos, we were surrounded by the everydayness of Earth—warm sunny days or cool fog, the oak rustling in the breeze, birds devouring seeds and insects, timid voles and darting lizards.

"I was the Clan Daughter," Breadbox sang, and Wanda translated to

English, "designated for a special role—poet-singer-chronicler. But special roles always meant unusual restrictions. Since poets and singers are by nature creative, unorthodox, breakers of rules, they also require stringent rules to channel their self-expression."

And Breadbox resisted. All young females rebelled and resisted, but she took it much farther than usual. "I should not have taken it so far—to the point where I failed to Choose my designated role. And now I have paid the price. My friends are dead on this unknown world, as beautiful as it is."

I need to give you a bit of background on her people, and a few of the real names, the way that Wanda, translating for Breadbox, rendered them to me.

Her real name was Bvar-nala-nga. Her people were the Hawfofonoloy. Haw was the name of her clan. Fofonoloy means "people of the world of Sfofong."

Now, I keep saying "people." But of course, these weren't people as in human beings—any more than Breadbox is a human being. We might view them as bug-eyed monsters. Breadbox used a term that has no English equivalent—no Earth equivalent. Sounded like "ohee" or "oki"—a bit like "oaky." It means any beings that have developed technology and can communicate with each other through symbolic means—i.e., language.

There's actually a subset of these oki, it turns out—those world races that can travel between stars and can make nice with each other and not exterminate, conquer, hunt down, or eat each other! And not mess with each other's worlds.

"It is against our rules to interfere with uncharted worlds like this one. This is why my clan forbade unauthorized trips like the one we took."

Breadbox described the Code of Oki, the basic rules of all the Confederation races. Reminded me of the Ten Commandments. One rule prohibited interfering with races that hadn't yet achieved high levels of technology. The reason was surprising: to maximize diversity. The worst thing would be to shape new races to be like the old races. Boring. Excitement comes from having very different societies and technologies. Kind of the opposite of our way of thinking.

"In times long past, my people, the Fofonoloy, had been explorers and inventors and experimenters and adventurers. We had explored many star systems and worlds. We had established a far-flung network of relationships for trade and knowledge exchange. We were an old people— one of the senior races in the Confederation of Oxygen-Breathing Peoples that stretches along one arm of the galaxy that contains our world.

"Our Elders always told us that we became too ambitious. Other worlds we visited felt encroached upon by the Fofonoloy. They resisted our advances. The Confederation forced my people to pull back into our own realm, and cease being so expansive.

"But I thought you told me the Confederation was all about expansion."

"Others expanded outward—to new worlds. My people expanded inward—toward worlds already occupied by oki civilizations."

She was silent for some time. "Another factor. Peoples of our body shape are less welcome. Most oki world races look more like people from your world—standing upright with four or six fixed appendages. These are Type 1 bodies, which evolved on solid surfaces. The Fofonoloy evolved on a wet world, in swamps and marshes. We have Type 2 bodies, with varying numbers of appendages, and without a solid skeleton."

"How many body types are there?"

"Four types on oxygen worlds. Type 3 beings live in the deep sea, and have appendages specialized for water. Type 4 live on dry land. They lack internal skeletons, but have an external hard structure.

"Type 4 sounds like bugs! I'm sorry to interrupt."

"I treasure your questions. What is a 'bugs?'"

"Bug. We see them all around us. That one is called a spider, this one buzzing around us is a fly. That blue one flying rapidly is called a dragonfly, and that shiny black one is a beetle. Some fly, some crawl. Six or eight legs.

"I see. On your world Type 4 is called 'bugs.' Our Type 4 races that are oki are larger. They have trouble communicating with Type 1 oki."

"Why were the Fofonoloy less welcome on other worlds?"

"Because we are different from most oki races. They are suspicious of us. We also communicate in a unique manner, mostly by singing. And we cannot eat the same food as others. Only Type 4 oki are viewed with more suspicion and hostility.

From what Breadbox was saying, it sounded like the wise, advanced galactic civilization had its own petty prejudices. Despite the Code of Oki valuing diversity, these oki still preferred beings that looked like themselves.

"I am so pleased that you treat me in a civilized manner, and not like some strange, fearful being."

"I suspect that many on my world would view you as a mon . . ." (No I didn't want to even suggest monster.) ". . . as strange and perhaps fearful."

"Perhaps because the Fofonoloy were looked down upon, we worked harder to show our superiority. I believe that our technologies and our devices, including this poor wrecked vessel, are considered superior. And perhaps this is why we were assertive with other world races."

"This would include your device I call Wanda?"

"Yes. If this were not true, how could three inexperienced youths be able to jump to distant worlds?"

Breadbox twittered and twitched nervously, and her skin patches rippled dark purple. "There is one additional factor I am ashamed to mention. My people, the Fofonoloy, brought a major problem upon ourselves. Many lifetimes in the past, our ancestors engaged in selective breeding to enhance desired traits and qualities, and this went on for a long time. In their hubris they 'played Creator' with the genome of our people. We had what you might call a 'genomic crash.' As a result, we must live partly within this metallic band to maintain our strength and longevity. Our Elders blamed this on prior generations of experimental scientists. The ensuing upheaval contributed to our move away from innovation and inventiveness.

"After that, a more conservative culture emerged. The message taught to our young became, 'The inventiveness of the past went too far. Too much newness is dangerous. It leads to longings that cannot be met. It created rifts within our society. We must live in cooperation with those around us on whom our well-being depends.' This is what we rebelled from."

Breadbox told me that this shift of culture had been pushed on the Fofonoloy by the conservative Confederation. Over time—centuries, if I am converting their time periods properly—they became ever more resistant to change. The new message became, "We must take the long view for the well-being of all."

History had been rewritten to distance the present from the creative, entrepreneurial past. "Our world had become a museum," Breadbox commented mournfully.

Creative self-expression was welcomed only if it led to no permanent change, but merely to trends or fashions or short-term belief systems. New technologies were allowed only if they increased comfort or safety or amusement. "Yet some sought to evade the shackles—my friends and I among them."

"What was it about you that made you more rebellious?" I asked.

"The young are naturally more adventurous. As I told you earlier, we Fofonoloy mature through several distinct physiological stages over our lifetime. Our behavior and attitudes shift with each stage, and so does our role in society.

"Young females, like me, newly emerging from juvenile status, are the creative drivers. Next, we become the mother-nurturers.

"In prior times," Breadbox went on, "the strongest bonds were often between a young female and a young male. They formed an ideal pair: she creative and inventive, he the engineer and organizer. But this is discouraged now."

"Why?" I asked.

"It could lead to dangerous paths of thinking and acting."

Thus males, in their current cultural milieu, were prevented from becoming entrepreneurs, and young females from being inventors or explorers, because the viewpoint of the clan society was that it didn't need more change or new things.

*   *   *

The next day it was my turn. I related my lifetime tale of triumph and woe. So paltry compared to her glorious leaps across the cosmos! But I'm not going to bore you with it. It's all there in the tabloids. True eternal love and love lost. Ah, Doug, where are you now? How I kept choosing the path to popularity and wealth, via shallowness, instead of putting out songs of deep meaning that nobody would pay to listen to.

Like Breadbox, I had chosen. And chosen wrong. Not once, but repeatedly. Like the time last year, in a pit of despond, I had called my old love Doug to see how he was doing. His wife (when did he get married?) answered and I could hear an infant and a small kid in the background. "I think you shouldn't call any more," she said politely, and I nodded my head in assent, my ears ringing with embarrassment.

Wait. I said I wasn't going to get into this. But Breadbox was fascinated. She ate this up. I, the poor native on a forlorn unknown world beyond the edge of her universe, had lived the life she craved.

Breadbox strongly disagreed that I had chosen the wrong path. And besides, she reminded me, since I had already chosen many times, I could still choose many more times. Unlike her, who only had one Choice, I had the freedom to choose a different path. Many times. Many times the choice would still face me. As often as the Moon rose.

10. The Restless Alien

I was beginning to understand more of Breadbox's singing and trumpeting without the intercession of Wanda. What was coming through loud and clear to me was that she wanted to get beyond her life-support tether, get out into the world and explore.

Several months had gone by since the crash and she was stir-crazy. She wanted to see more. She was full of questions about our world—questions I didn't have answers to. I was spending a good bit of time on the internet, educating myself so that I could give meaningful answers.

But talking wasn't enough. She wanted to see things. But how?

Her vessel was up a steep, rocky hill, then down in a gully, reached by a path not that easy even for an agile human being to navigate. She had stubby little legs. I had no idea how she would do, having to clamber over rocks to get to where I could park my Jeep.

Plus, she spent a lot of time connected to her life-support system. True, she was getting stronger, and she was now able to scurry around the vicinity of the vessel without the connecting tube. But now she was talking about field trips!

She wanted to see how I live. How could I get her up the gulch, then down to my house? How long could she safely be off her life support? Could she scurry on her pseudopod legs? Could I carry her? Could I put her in the wheelbarrow? Or in my little red wagon that I use for garden work? She wasn't very big, but she was compact and heavy. I remember the time I had to carry Buddy back to my place after he tangled with the coyote. She was heavier than that.

It turned out my wheelbarrow worked best—after Clay and I spent a couple of hours filling in holes to make a path for the wheel. Poor Clay! I used up most of my brownie points with him, plus some poor-weak-woman wheedling, to get him to help me hack and shovel and tamp dirt and small rocks into place. He definitely earned his steak dinner and Malbec that evening.

I could tip up the wheelbarrow, and she'd climb in, then cling to the sides. My biceps and triceps got a major workout pushing her up the hill to where my Jeep awaited. But she loved the ride. Who wouldn't? I sure did when I was a little girl.

In my Jeep, I built a makeshift platform above my back seat, then rigged up a ramp with two landscaping boards, so she could scramble up into the back.

I drove her down the steep hill to my house, bumping over the rocks and erosion gullies. I showed her all through my house, explaining what I did in each room. The things that fascinated her the most were the toilet (apparently she uses a very different approach), my shower (she wanted to try it!), and food. She watched every detail while I fixed Clay and me a steak dinner and as we ate it. I had trouble explaining smell to her; maybe she doesn't even have a sense of smell.

"I wish I could try your food!"

"Is there a way this can happen?"

"I must eat only the food that is produced by the vessel and fed to me through the apparatus you have seen."

"How long can you be away from it?"

"Now that I am regaining my strength, I need be connected to it only a part of each day-night cycle."

"What happens if that food on your vessel runs out?"

"It won't run out. The vessel grows its own food inside the tank, specially created for our bodies' nutritional needs."

"Are you worried about contracting any kind of disease from microorganisms on our world?"

"My device has analyzed your air and water and bits of soil and found them to be safe for me, or else it created an anti-microbe substance to protect me. Whenever my people travel to different worlds, we must also make sure we bring with us no toxins or microbes that could damage them. When we crashed, I was glad to learn that our instruments that analyzed

Breadbox wanted to see more of the world.

45

substances on your world still functioned and determined that we would bring nothing harmful to you. Partly this is because our anatomy is so different. But also, our vessels contain miniscule anti-microbe beings that continually scour for potentially harmful organisms."

It sounded like an immune system for a machine. This actually lifted a huge load off my mind. Assuming it was true. Well, no galactic hungy-fungy yet.

She loved my music collection. We played the stereo with volume turned up on all four speakers. She thrummed and vibrated, learned the melodies, sang along. She loved my songs most, I'm tickled to say, and on subsequent visits, she learned to sing along with me. I did the lyrics, she sang the melody—several voices at once. Best backup I ever had!

She was enthralled by TV, and it may have been a mistake to teach her how to use the remote. But why was it so flat, she wondered? She wanted to be able to reach into it. While watching a news broadcast, she asked, "Can they see us?" The lack of two-way, 3D television did not stop her from devouring hours of cartoons and nature shows and old sci-fi movies.

She dug my bugs and worms. Beneath my kitchen sink, I keep a bucket for organic garbage to be buried in my garden compost heap. Digging into the compost heap to bury the garbage revealed hundreds of earthworms, pill bugs, ants, centipedes, and various other creepy-crawlies. She was fascinated. She crawled right into the compost heap to commune with the Earth beings that were closest to her anatomically. Had her kind descended from centipede-like creatures? I wondered.

Each evening, I had to get her back to her vessel and life support before it got too dark for me to navigate the narrow path with the wheelbarrow. But it was difficult to pull her away.

She soon learned to climb up into the back of the Jeep without the ramp. I moved the wheelbarrow up to the side of the Jeep. She would stand on her "hind legs," reach up with her "arms," and pull herself up. I've seen caterpillars and worms stand like this and reach out across a void. She looked for all the world like a larger version of that.

11. Sweet Stuff Singer

Cotton candy lovin'
You get your cotton candy
At the circus of life
From "Cotton Candy Lovin'" on Selena M's Classics album

Morty called to make sure I was going to show up for my gig, and I took the opportunity to moan a little bit.

"Morty, Morty. Oh lordy, I'm forty!"

"Well, maybe you can do a comeback tour. Get over it. Get a face-lift. You don't look so bad." This was his idea of a pep talk.

"Comeback tour? I'm not even gone yet."

"Yeah? You will be if you miss any of these gigs I'm lining up for you."

"I'll be there." I immediately ran to the mirror. Did I really need a face-lift?

I felt guilty about leaving my guest. "I'll be away for a short while this evening. I have to do this thing." I apologized profusely.

"I will sing to the stars, awaiting your return. What must you do that is so unpleasant?"

"I have to sing to some people."

Breadbox was fascinated. She was very interested in me going out to sing. "Why are you not happy? You are a singer. You are doing what you love, what you are meant to do."

She wanted to hear what I was going to sing. I promised to sing them all for her the next day.

*   *   *

Getting to Sonoma State campus is just an hour's drive through peaceful dairy-farm country on a gorgeous late-summer afternoon. I hummed my songs and practiced my patter. This wouldn't be so bad. I arrived in a pretty good mood. I grabbed Gibb and went into the auditorium to set up. My guess was that the parents would know my music and their freshman kids would have no idea who I was.

I stood on the stage looking out over this multi-generational audience. When I was starting out, these moms were the age of their daughters. So was I. Oh, my, don't go there, I thought to myself. Just start singing.

Gibb and my fingers knew what to do.

Cotton candy lovin', that's all I seem to find
It makes you high, that sugar lovin' kind.
But soon I crash, I hit the floor
It leaves me hungry, wantin' more

I search again, to see who I can find.
Just another sugar lovin' kind.
That's cotton candy love, but I don't mind.

The moms sang along—even some of the dads. I was surprised to see a lot of the daughters getting into it. The sons, not so much.

Very gratifying applause, even though nobody got up and danced in the aisles.

Afterward a middle-aged woman (Yikes! My age? Do I look like her?!) came up and introduced her daughter Mandy to me. Mandy was very shy. "You've always been a role model to Mandy. You are so out there, but you are also accessible, approachable. I just wanted her to see you up close."

"Hi, Mandy. Are you a singer?"

She shook her head yes, then no. "But could I have your autograph?" she asked softly, without quite looking me in the eye.

"Yes, you may. But on one condition: only if I can also have your autograph." She looked directly at me with astonishment. "And, I want you to promise that you will get up and sing a song in front of others. Write that down with that autograph."

She did this! She promised. Gave it to me in writing. I could see the smile of a singer peeping out from behind her shy eyes. Her mother gushed her gratitude.

Well, that made me feel good. Then a college-age guy came up and asked me how much I charge for an autograph. "I'll pay you a buck to take one!" I retorted. He didn't get it. What kind of a celebrity would do that? He walked away looking confused. Maybe he figured that if I was so hard up I'd pay him, he wouldn't be able to resell it for much.

*   *   *

When I got home, I trekked up to the crash site to check on my favorite alien, carrying my big, bright flashlight. Breadbox was in the opening of the vessel, singing softly and swaying.

She was eager to see me. "What did you sing tonight? Could you sing it to me?"

"Just my standard songs," I said, dripping with unenthusiasm. I was in no mind to start singing just then.

"You sound not happy. Why is that?"

Grumble. Mutter.

"Why are you a singer?"

"It's a living. A thing I do to amuse myself."

"People want to hear you sing. You sing their stories."

I flashed on drunks talking noisily at the bar during my gigs, and me trying to sing over them, drown them out.

"A singer is a very high calling," Breadbox said. "On my world, only very special people are selected for this honor. Were you chosen to be a singer? Or did you choose it yourself?"

"I kind of fell into it. It just happened."

I didn't feel like being probed on my career just then. So I turned the question on her. "You also were chosen to be a singer, and you refused your choice.

"I was required to sing songs of little passion. Lessons for the young. To convey the favored stories of our Elders, passed down over the years. And the stories contained untruths. Just a single style of music, repeated endlessly.

"Singing just a single note is dull and boring. The mingled notes make a pleasing whole. Drawing with one tentacle is boring. Many intertwined lines emerging together make a pleasing whole. A person doing one thing in life is boring. Many interests—some pulling together, others pulling apart—make a pleasingly whole person.

"Singing must be an act of creation. On my world, in my song, my dance, I would be expected to present myself to others as somebody else, someone of a time long past, and that is how they would see me. Not as myself. I wanted to sing my own song. This is why I refused my Choice."

She tilted her eyestalks toward me. "You have the freedom to sing your own song, yet you do not."

We both sat quietly for a while, musing on weird fate. Then she said, "I refused my calling as a singer. You seem to go sing only with reluctance. Yet we both sing joyously with each other."

It was after midnight when I headed back down the hill, in a deep funk. I felt like I had missed my chance, by not taking my singing seriously all these years. And now it was too late. I was sliding over the hill and down the other side.

Why am I a singer? I asked myself. I was practically crying. Clearly not because my parents wanted me to be. They wanted me to go into the sciences. Perhaps medicine, although since I was a girl, they'd probably thought nursing. But then my brother, who's a year older than me, got drafted out of college to play baseball. In his typical big brother mode, he taunted me, "You know, Bertie, this is something only guys can do . . ."

"Don't call me Bertie!" This was when I had just decided to go by Selena, not Berthe. He ignored this interruption of his taunt.

". . . There's no way girls can get drafted out of college to do something that makes them filthy rich."

I took that as a dare. I had been working with this little band that we called Tres Chick, making spoof songs and singing them on campus, so I decided to record one of them. That was "Cotton Candy Lovin'," and it became the signature hit on my first album. Shortly after, I left school to go on tour, just like my big brother had, and never went back. It was a "nya nya nya nya nya nya nya" moment.

My poor brother never made it to the majors. He played a couple of years in minor leagues, and then got a job selling insurance. He's done well for himself in insurance, but it's not "the big show."

My parents never came around to accept my music career. My dad says, "Yeah, you've done well, but you could've made a much bigger contribution to the world in medicine. Even as a nurse." And for my mom, bless her heart, the most devastating thing was that I blew my chance of getting married, and hadn't had any strong relationships since then.

"What good is all that wealth you have without a husband and children to share it with?" I learned long ago not even to respond to comments like this.

Fortunately, when my brother got married and produced a couple of grandkids for them, it took some of the pressure off me.

So, true confessions time. Singing was no high-flown calling, no honor bestowed on me, no passion from my heart. It was a dare from my brother, to show I could make more money than he did. Breadbox had entirely the wrong idea about me.

*　　*　　*

The next day, Sunday, I brought Breadbox down to my house. We brought her drawing gear so she could sketch things around my place.

Breadbox had sketched half a flip-chart pad of work, from doodles to intricate drawings. Her technique was improving with all the practice. She had graduated from felt-tip markers to a set of colored charcoals I had bought for her. Some of her work was beginning to look like impressionist pieces. There was one of me sitting beneath the big oak that was reminiscent of the technique of my namesake, Berthe Morisot.

"What is a 'namesake'?" she asked me.

"Somebody you were named for. My real name, given me by my family, is Berthe. Berthe Morisot Monahan." As I tell all who ask, that's "Bear-tuh" please, not "Birth-a."

"So you have three names: Selena, the singer; Agate, name given by me; and now I learn Berthe, given by your clan. Is that a secret name?"

"No, not secret. Just not preferred by me. My mother named me after an artist, Berthe Morisot, whom she studied in school. Morisot lived in France, the homeland of my mother. Some of your drawings remind me of hers.

"I wish I could see some of her paintings."

I hauled down the big art book that my mother had given me, showing many of Morisot's paintings. We leafed through the book, and I showed

Breadbox how her drawings were similar to Morisot's impressionist works. "Berthe Morisot was the only woman painter among a circle of men," I explained.

"You also have a circle of men."

"Yes, that's true." I wondered how Morisot got on with all these other male artists, including her husband. Nineteenth-century Frenchmen. Could have been a handful.

Breadbox was carefully leafing through the book. It looked to me like she had little suction cups on the ends of her tentacles she was using as fingers. I'd never noticed that before. Sure came in handy to turn pages. "I love these. I want to draw like these. She captures the real life of these people. And the places they live. She must paint from her heart. The woman in this painting looks like you."

"That one has always been my favorite."

I loved Morisot's paintings, but I dumped her first name way back in high school, and kept her last. I had always loved gazing at the Moon. My mother said I was always mooning around. My boyfriend—was that Geoff?—called me his moon goddess. That's Selena. It stuck with me as soon as I started college. Half my classmates were the children of hippies who had strange names, so I fit right in. Born Berthe Morisot Monahan, I became Selena Morisot. My first agent shortened it to Selena M. For marketing purposes, of course.

*   *   *

That night Berthe Morisot spoke to me. It was a vivid dream. She wore a painter's smock over her blue cotton dress, and had her hair pulled into a bun. She showed me a painting she was working on, pointing with a long, thin brush she held in her hand. She spoke in French, which I understood, but then repeated it in accented English, so I would be sure to get it. "I always paint from my heart. I always paint from my heart." She looked directly at me. "Only painting from the heart is alive; anything else is flat and dead. Painting is like music. To be pleasing, there must be rhythm and harmony; otherwise it is chaos and cacophony. When do the jangling notes become a pleasing whole?"

With her long paintbrush, she pointed out symbols on the canvas that I'd never before noticed. She turned back to her canvas and continued working. She sang a little tune, painting while she sang. I woke up humming that tune.

I fumbled for the recorder I keep beside my bed, and turned it on to capture this melody, humming in the wee hours before it evaporated with the sunrise.

"Always play from the heart." Easy for her to say.

12. Agate and Breadbox's Great Adventure

A dog is a man's best friend
My best friend is an alien.
From Inner-Galactic Journey album

From my deck, Breadbox could see the ocean. We had often watched sailboats and fishing boats, large container ships in the distance, and even the occasional brave cluster of ocean kayakers. She wanted to go to the beach. "Are you allowed to go to the edge of the water?" she asked.

I said, "Of course! There are beaches covered with sand. We can get into the water if we want." I showed her my surfboard, which I hadn't used for at least ten years.

"On my world, we also have oceans, but we are not allowed to go near them." She waved her tentacles to imitate the waves on the sea. "That is the realm of the beings that live there. The oceans are reserved for the sea creatures; it is not for us to encroach upon them.

"There are old myths about our kind swimming across bodies of water, with only our eyes and mouths above the surface. But now the Elders frighten us with tales of large, untamed beasts that would devour us in the deep water. And it's considered an invasion of their realm. Just like we were not supposed to invade your realm, but we did. We've paid the price for breaking the rules." She said this with a slump of sadness.

What she said astounded me. It was as if we decided that the Pacific Ocean was reserved for the dolphins and whales and we were no longer allowed to sail upon the sea, because they are intelligent beings, and there's no justification for us to trespass on their waters. No doubt there are people on our world who would applaud that.

"Breadbox, how then do you know about agates? How many beaches on different worlds have you seen?

"I have ambled slowly along the beaches on my home world, looking with longing out across the huge water. Bright sands at the beginning of day, nearly untrodden, my kind never go there any more. Beaches are deserted, I am alone. I see the vastness of sand littered with bits of things washed up by the sea. And so rarely, the beautiful, round, golden stone illuminated by the rising sun."

How could I take her to the beach? I wasn't eager to show off my visitor to all the tourists driving up and down Highway 1. But she was as insistent as a young kid. I explained the situation to her, embarrassed that she might feel insulted. But she agreed with me not to be revealed and stared at by all manner of strangers.

So we worked out a way. I put her in the back seat with blankets piled up and wrapped her so that there was nothing showing but her eyestalks.

I must confess that I didn't even tell my friends about this outing, for fear they'd talk me out of it.

Oh, another thing! Breadbox couldn't handle bright sunlight. That's often the least of our problems here along the foggy coastline. But we were having glorious, sunny late-summer days. So we did our first venture out at dusk. I headed up the coast a bit to a secluded public beach, where I could drive right to the edge of the sand. This had always been Buddy's favorite beach.

She was definitely not satisfied to sit and look. She climbed over the edge of the Jeep and had just enough stretch in her tentacles to reach the ground.

I'm an ambler. Buddy, my old dog, would bound and leap and chase the Frisbee into the surf. Breadbox scurried. I don't know how else to describe it! She was like a turbo-charged caterpillar. She resembled a small army tank when she ran around. Not good on dry sand, but on the wet sand where the waves wash in, she could move quite rapidly.

At the south end of this beach at low tide are some tide pools, inaccessible enough so that they're not picked clean by the tourists. She waded right in and was instantly fascinated by the shore life she saw as I highlighted them with my big flashlight. Hermit crabs, starfish, anemones, sea urchins, small fish darting around. She was as delighted and inquisitive as a kindergartner. I was afraid she would wash out to sea, but it turned out she could swim! Just like her ancestors.

I delighted in watching her, even though I kept glancing back toward the parking lot, paranoid that others would arrive and see her here.

She picked up a collection of beach treasures—a sand dollar; a piece of green glass worn smooth as a pebble, probably from a broken bottle; and an agate. A deep-amber piece of agate, about a centimeter across. She held it up and presented it to me. I was moved to tears. Later, I had it mounted and put it on a small chain alongside the amulet. (I'm wearing it even now.)

As we headed back to my Jeep, this guy I hadn't seen yelled, "Hey lady! Your dog's supposed to be on a leash!" I waved, said thank you, and hurried toward the Jeep. He hollered after us, "Say, what kind of dog is that, anyway?" I yelled over my shoulder, "It's an Asian wolfhound," and shepherded Breadbox around to the other side of the Jeep. Fortunately, he was more interested in his own six-pack. Yikes! That was a close one. Breadbox looks nothing like a dog. I guess when someone sees her in poor light, their eyes want to make her into something recognizable.

Later, I realized with horror that I had taken a being that lived inside a metal cummerbund to go swimming in the salty ocean. Would she rust or corrode shut, like the Tin Man in The Wizard of Oz? When we got home, I led her into my house, leaving a trail of sand across the floor, and took her into the shower. I showered her down with warm water, using the hose attachment to get her underside. She loved this! Then, I toweled her off like I would a large dog and used my hairdryer to dry her off, taking care not to scorch her bare skin. The things we do for our favorite aliens!

It was after 11 pm, so I had to take her down the hill in the wheelbarrow in the pitch dark. I asked her to hold my big flashlight so I could see where I was going. But of course, she was turning it every which way. I wondered if she could catch poison oak.

This outing established a precedent, because she now wanted to go more places. My secret alien wanted me to take her out into the wider world. How long could I put her off, I wondered?

Breadbox finds a kindred being.

13. Berzerkly

Apparently the floodgates had opened. Morty called and said, "We've got another gig for you in Berkeley."

I kept getting sucked back into the money game. Here's how it worked. Morty calls, insists that I take some gig, sing my old standards. I object, then grudgingly agree. Is this fitting behavior for somebody who has been chosen to be a singer?

Morty channels this money-driven side of me. You've seen people with a little devil sitting on one shoulder, an angel on the other, each trying to influence them. Morty whispers right into my ear. Whispers? No, yells.

"You better keep on the road, girl! You're not getting any younger. You let down now and you'll never bounce back. Maybe as a gray-haired lady with a cane doing a comeback tour. No, you don't want that. Stay in it. Sell what people are buying. They don't want deep, meaningful, uplifting lyrics. They want you to resonate with their poor, loveless lives."

The problem was, I had no angel sitting on the other shoulder to counter this message. Until Breadbox. Her life was her message. "Go for what you want. The hell with the critics." Actually, I didn't know whether she ever swore. Note to self: Learn some of her galactic swear words.

"This gig is at Berzerkly. You've done that before. They like your sound, but they don't want to hear all your old music—they wanna know if you have anything new."

"Morty, I've got what I've got." I couldn't believe I heard myself saying that, since I've been berating Morty for touting me as a comfortable oldies singer.

"They say you could play some covers of others, and they've got suggestions of what they'd like."

"So now they're telling the musicians what to play?"

"Hey, they're givin' you the gold—you do as you're told."

That really made me angry. What do they want me to do—write a whole bunch of new music just for this one gig? It wasn't that much money. On the other hand, maybe I could work in a couple of these tunes I'd been playing around with.

*   *   *

It's way too far to drive home to the coast from Berkeley after a late-night gig. I would have to stay overnight there. That meant finding a babysitter—somebody to look in on Breadbox during the evening. Clay couldn't do it that evening.

"Doc, big favor. I need a baby sitter. I've got to go sing some sweet music in Berkeley, and I'm wondering if you would be willing to look in on our patient while I'm gone."

"You want me to camp out there overnight?"

"No, no. Just look in on her sometime during the evening. Make sure she doesn't get tangled up in her feeding tube, or whatever."

"Won't be the first time I've babysat some iffy beast late at night. I charge double time for that."

"Put it on my tab." I was sure glad he wasn't charging me for all the time he was putting in.

Berzerkly is right near the UC Berkeley campus on Telegraph. It wasn't my usual crowd at all. Younger, hipper. Martinis and merlot, not beer and tequila. This club had the rep of bringing in radical, avant-garde artists, which meant a lot of weird music. What am I going to play?

I started with this newish one that was more reminiscent of John Denver than my typical country rock sound.

> *Please take care of my heart, love*
> *while I'm a thousand miles away.*
> *You know how much I love you*
> *Even though I cannot stay.*
>
> *Nurture our love*
> *Keep it strong*
> *I'll be back before too long*
>
> *Even when we're far apart*
> *Off in my city head, neglecting my heart*
> *I rely on you to hold us as one, dear*
> *Don't let my long travels pull us asunder.*

They liked it! They liked it a lot. Do I dare play a first-timer?

"Thank you, thank you! Last time I was here—this was before the new owner, thank you Gregory—the guy said, 'You can't expect to get top billing, you're just a girl.' Oh, did that piss me off! Yeah I'm a girl, but I'm Super Girl! Right here in these fingers I have a deadly weapon. My guitar pick. I will play you down into the ground." That got me a standing ovation. "That inspired this next song. I call it Anthem to My Secret Self."

I started off soft, like a ballad:

> *If the world only knew me*
> *And knew what I could do*
> *If the world could only see me*
> *And appreciate the view*
> *No scoffing, "She's just a girl."*

I followed this with a strident guitar riff to express my pissed-off-ness at being unappreciated. Then into the second verse.

> *Inside I'm a hero*
> *I often save the world*
> *I smite the bad guys, save the good*
> *Pretty good for just a girl!*
> *Thank you, Super Girl!*

"Pretty good for just a girl! Come on, sing along, everybody, especially you girls out there. Pretty good for just a girl. Thank you, Super Girl!"
Then softer again.

> *My inner self's a beauty*
> *When will I show the world?*
> *But I'm afraid you'll brush me off*
> *Or ignore me, even worse.*
> *Scoffing, "She's just a girl."*

Finally, a big finish.

> *I honor myself; it's time to shine*
> *To do what I can do*
> *To tell my truth, to claim what's mine*
> *To sing my inner song to you*
> *And sing my inner song*
> > *The song of Super Girl*

No question, this was the right venue to introduce that song!

During the applause, I flashed on my visitor hidden away in the hill up behind my house, and her songs about all the worlds she knew, and her song to our world here. Without even thinking, I played the riff on my guitar. The tune rolled out past my mind's ear, and my fingers just started playing it.

"I'm going to call this Song to Home." Very soft, just guitar, me humming along, slow and reverent. I choked up halfway through.

Couldn't go on for a minute. They had to bring me a box of tissues from offstage.

When I finished, people remained silent for a moment. Nobody did anything. I thought, "Wow did I bomb!" Then there was just a huge burst of applause. People yelled and asked for an encore. I didn't have an encore; I just sat there on the stool. This was the first time this had ever happened to me. I dared to put it all out there, and they loved it.

A woman came up to me afterwards and said, "I didn't know whether I should applaud or not. It felt like you were singing a hymn, like we were in church. What album is that on?"

"It's not even recorded yet. This is the first time I've played it."

Another guy came up and said, "You never played anything like that before. That's not your music—you musta stole that offa somebody."

I stared at him blankly. "Yeah, I guess that's kind of true," I said half to myself. "Don't know whether you'd call it theft. She probably would approve. I guess I gotta check that out."

Another guy pushed his way through the crowd, saying, "Hey, what was that little riff you did there? I'd like to hear more of that. Never heard you play anything like that before."

"Oh, just my fingers fooling around."

"Well, if your fingers decide to fool around that way for a few more bars, I would love to get a disk from you. Might be interested in recording that."

"And who are you, sir? I don't think we've met."

"I'm Joel. I produce music."

Selena gets up the nerve to play music she's never dared share before.

What a heartthrob! Would I throw over my label for him?

I stayed at a small hotel just off Telegraph. I didn't get to sleep till after 3 am. Couldn't get Joel out of my mind. And it wasn't about recording my music.

I fell asleep exhausted, but woke up a bit later. The song was coursing through my mind. I had no option but to get up and scratch it down. Play it and record it and scratch it down. That's the way songs happen. When the creative urge comes along, catch it by the tail. Not that I was ever going to do anything with this, but still.

I had breakfast at Yoga and Waffles on Durant before heading home. I about jumped out of my chair when Joel from last night came in. What a hunk! Would he go for somebody like me? Well, here he was. But he wanted to talk music. "No, I don't want to compete with your label. I just want to record it, produce it. Keep it simple. No big embellishments. I loved the way you crooned without words. But I'd also love a few lines of lyrics just to set the tone."

Umm, he smelled so good. "Joel, want to come out to my studio on the coast and have a private session?" I did not say this, alas.

He made no move on me and I headed back home alone. I felt the futility of inviting him to visit.

Was I ever again going to have romance in my life? I'd had my doubts lately, but Joel definitely rekindled the feelings. Alas, it would not be this day. "Joel darling, I want to introduce you to my housemate Breadbox." Or perhaps, "I've got to duck out for a minute and go take care of the little old creature I keep locked in a tin shed up the hill. Be right back." Guaranteed to dampen ardor.

But hey, we had set a date for a recording session in the city.

*   *   *

This whole episode just brought home to me how lonely I have been. I have numbed myself to passion and romance.

But this wasn't really true. I had friends, even boy friends. Clay, Jim (well, he's married), Doc, whom I'd really only gotten to know since Breadbox arrived.

What about Clay? He was too . . . too what? Too unexciting? For an old chick, ready to settle down into comfortable oblivion, he'd be the perfect man. But was I ready for that? I sometimes thought I might be. But my spirit, my juices, had been roused. By this crazy alien interloper. Loping into my life, stirring things up. I was stirred up. And by this guy in Berkeley who liked her crazy music and wanted to record it.

What would happen next? I didn't know. But not the same ole, same ole.

I went back home early next morning, after hardly any sleep, to check on my charge in the damaged tin can. I was wiped out, but not so wiped that I didn't check over every figure on the term sheet and pay summary, and see that all the stuff had actually been transferred to my account. Every dang cent less Morty's rake-off.

I played this new song to Breadbox. She jumped right into the music and created a whole 'nother verse—just made it up on the spot.

I went back and listened to my recording of all the little ditties she had sung the first night we sat out under the stars, for all the different worlds in her universe. I thought, "You know, these could be strung together. I could call it the 'Galaxy Suite.' Would I be stealing these from Breadbox? I'd better ask her."

"Breadbox, when you and I sing, you inspire me to create new music. Then I go and play it to other people. Would you think I was taking something that was yours?" She looked at me, didn't quite understand for a moment until I said it a different way.

Her response to me was, "Take me with you! I want to hear it!"

14. Men Fight Over Me

The following morning, as I returned from a shopping trip to Bodega Bay and chugged up the steep hill of my driveway in my Jeep, I saw Doc and Clay engaging in fisticuffs. Flailing at each other. Their shoving and yelling match was taking place right in front of Breadbox, who was in the wheelbarrow.

I sprayed gravel, got up to the top as fast as I could, pulled on the brake, and jumped out. "Boys, boys, what is going on here!?"

Just then, the wheelbarrow tipped over, spilling Breadbox onto the gravel. She landed on her side, but quickly righted herself. This got their attention, and Doc ran to her. The patches on her skin were pulsing vivid colors. This must have scared the bejeebers out of her.

Doc had a bruise on his cheek, which could well develop into a black eye. "This yoyo is jealous that you asked me, rather than him, to babysit our alien visitor."

These two grown men got in a fight—over me!

"Oh guys, this is ridiculous! Clay, I asked Doc because his medical knowledge might be very important should something happen with Breadbox. And besides, you'll recall you were in a teacher's conference that evening. This is no statement about our friendship."

I turned my attention to Breadbox. "How does she happen to be here?"

Doc tattled. "Clay wheeled her down here."

Clay looked sheepish. "She wanted to look at your art books. She told me using her talking tube. So I brought her down here. I didn't think you would mind."

"Are you hurt?" I asked her.

"Not hurt. Anxious about fighting." she said.

"Yes, I can imagine."

They were solicitous toward Breadbox, but still pissed at each other. Like two squabbling brothers. I could see it was going to take more to mollify them, so I said, "My Berzerkly gig night before last went really well, and I'd love to tell you guys about it. Could I fix a steak dinner for both of you this evening?"

Clay glowered and Doc shook his head. "You two need a night together."

"I'll pass," grumbled Clay.

"You idiots, you can sit on opposite sides of the room. You don't have to eat any of my delicious steak or drink any of my wine, but I want to tell you what happened in Berkeley." Leaving out the part about Joel, of course.

Before they could object, I pulled the bottle of red wine out of my shopping bag and held it up. "Look, it's a Carmenere, very highly rated. I need somebody to help me check it out." I could see wavering in their reluctance. "7:30 this evening. Now get out of here. But first, I want both of you to apologize to Breadbox." They did so, but with reluctance and discomfort. Was it the idea of apologizing to a non-human creature?

As they headed separately down my driveway, I had a very unworthy thought comparing Joel to Clay. "But Clay fought over me. Crazy, distressing. Yet exciting!"

15. Bloody Murder

"I am so sorry you saw Clay and Doc fighting in front of you. You looked frightened." I wanted to pick her up in my arms, like a frightened child. Totally impractical.

"It surprised me. Worried that they might hurt each other. Were they fighting for your favor?"

"So it seems. Surprised me, too." I couldn't suppress a small smile at the thought.

Breadbox and I were back near her vessel. She disconnected from her feeding tube, climbed down off the gurney and trundled out through the gash in the side of the vessel. She climbed up on a small boulder in the shade of the oak tree. I pulled my chair over beside her to continue our conversation.

"Do fights like this ever take place among your people?" I asked her.

"On our world we have dances that simulate fighting. Some are stylized re-enactments of ancient struggles. Some are serious competitions."

"Yes, we do that on Earth also. I wonder if re-enacting old wars keeps new ones from popping up. We haven't had a war in this country for a long time."

"Our kind used to fight," she said. "But it is now forbidden, strongly discouraged."

"How do your kind fight?" I asked.

"Entangle our tentacles. Grasp each other's eyestalks. Try to make the other fall or surrender. Hold the opponent down. Trying to establish dominance, not inflict injury."

"Wrestling, we call that."

"We fear injury, death, humiliation, grudges," she said.

As we watched, the local cat that had been hanging around leapt after a small animal in the grass that it had been stalking. Didn't catch it.

Breadbox had a certain way of waving two of her tentacles when she was about to explain some foible of her people. "We have tried to ban death. The eldest often die hidden away. They go on a 'trip' and never return."

"So old Fofonoloy just disappear instead of dying with their clan? That surprises me. There's no honoring of their life and friendship?"

She twisted her body and looked away from me, toward the graves of her crewmembers. "Oh, yes, there is, but only some time after they have passed away."

"Death and anger and struggle are integral to your society," she said softly. It sounded strange on this gorgeous sunny day that was bursting with life at every level.

"Alas, yes."

"That is as it should be," she said. "The idea of 'no death' is an illusion. A dangerous illusion."

I had never before had a discussion like this with anybody.

"Death as a gift," she said. "I have experienced this here."

"A gift?"

"The four-legged fur-covered semi-oki that visits and speaks."

"Ah, the cat we just saw. I think it belongs to Jed up the hill. This is its territory."

"Yes. Cat. It brought me a part of a smaller beast. Left it next to my gurney. I perceived it as a gift or offering."

"Yes, my old dog Buddy once brought a chicken home and put it on the floor in front of me. Seemed like an offering. Unfortunately I had to punish him, to make him know he could not do this, because dogs that kill chickens are themselves killed by the angry owners of the chickens. I had to figure out whose chicken it was, and apologize, and buy them a new chicken."

"I watch the black flying beasts. They give each other pieces of small beings, dead."

"Crows."

"They work together and talk with each other constantly. They must be oki. My device here that you call Wanda is trying to decipher their language and compile a lexicon."

The crows strutted and hopped around in the grass near us, pecking things out of the ground, bugs I guess, talking constantly. Some sounded like they were talking cooperatively and others on tree limbs cawed stridently. Sounded to me like, "Mine's bigger than yours!" "Oh yeah? Mine's bigger!"

Suddenly there was a huge ruckus about fifteen yards up toward the poison oak patch. A hawk—red tail I believe—had swooped out of the sky and attacked one crow on the ground that was separated a bit from the others. The hawk pinned the crow to the ground and was eating it while it was still alive. Pecking its guts out. The other crows were in an uproar, circling around the hawk, screaming, but not getting too close. The hawk crouched over the crow, wings spread like a blanket to keep all others away from its meal, and making this fierce growling sound I'd never before heard from a bird.

I was astounded to hear Wanda begin saying words in English, apparently translating what the crows were saying. "No! Stop! Fear!" "We will kill you!"

But these were empty threats. The crows were not about to attack the hawk. Very soon, the downed crow was dead. The hawk calmly continued eating it while the other crows looked on. They got silent, watched for a short while, and then one by one flew away. That was the end of it.

The hawk ate its fill, cleaned its beak and its feathers a bit, walked around, then took off. The crows started yelling at it again. Some chased it away, but much too late. Before long, a turkey buzzard flew into view and circled, but was unwilling to approach because we were too close.

Breadbox was trembling violently. The color patches on her skin went bright scarlet. I thought she was having a seizure. Maybe she was. I had done this to her. I was horror stricken that I had exposed her to these episodes of violence and death. She slowly stopped shaking but her tentacles did this rapid, intricate dance of their own.

We just sat in stunned silence for a while, letting it sink in. "This is a story of your world," Breadbox said. "This is the way things work on your world. I think they work like this on most worlds. But we have been shielded from it on our world. All such interactions are far outside of where we live. We do not see such things. But here, right where you live, we have seen several different levels of one being killing and eating another, and even eating live beings.

It surprised me that so soon after this horrifying event, Breadbox was philosophizing about it. She turned things to philosophical lessons the way I turn things to music.

"In the history of our Confederation, our first rule is 'Do not eat each other.'"

"Why is this the very first rule? You have told me that these are highly civilized, highly advanced world races."

"Because in early times we did kill and eat each other. Different world races would go to other worlds and hunt down the beings that lived there, kill them, and eat them for meat. Of course, we did many other negative things as well. Enslave one another. Just kill others for sport. Or for no particular reason, just for fighting over something. Getting very different world races to abide to basic rules like these has allowed us to develop a shared civilization."

I nodded agreement. "Doesn't sound much different than us. On our world, we also have a code of behavior similar to your Code of Oki. The first rule is 'Thou shalt not kill.' It is a widely ignored rule. There are many excuses for when it is appropriate and acceptable—and even required—to kill one another. This rule applies only to our own kind. And most definitely does not restrict us from killing other types of beings on this world—nor forbid other beings from killing each other."

Suddenly I froze in terror. Petrified, I looked upward as a small plane flew almost directly overhead, paralleling the coastline. What if the pilot saw us—or at least the crashed vessel—and called it in?

Breadbox picked up on my strong emotional reaction. She climbed

65

down off the rock—surprisingly agile I would say—went into her vessel, and connected herself to her life support or feeding tube. I feared this conversation was taking too much out of her. But she went on, speaking from the inner sanctum of her dark vessel, via Wanda.

"Competition, struggle, death. Communication, communion, and connection. These are universals. We must accommodate them." This sounded like she was repeating a lesson she had been taught. "That is one message I was meant to communicate by my singing. That is valid. I did not object to singing these themes, only the way I would be required to sing them."

She went on with her little lecture. "People want to live and they fear death, so they seek to change their very beings so that they will live forever—or at least for a very long time. Races have tried to banish death.

"We experimented with our genetic basis too much and that's why I, and most others, have to wear these metal bands around our middle, to actually hold ourselves together, because we bred weakness into ourselves."

I moved my chair over nearer the opening in the spaceship so I could hear her better. She went on. "While we all like to live, one can see that in the big picture, death is essential, both to avoid overcrowding and for renewal."

"I am anxious for the future of my people, and of many world races in the Confederation. We strongly need to renew the vigor and vitality. Instead, I see a spreading stagnation, lethargy. Beings, and entire world races, with limited energy and excitement." Her skin patches turned the darkest maroon I had ever seen on her.

"As my race has gotten older, they increasingly forbade the kind of exploring that we engaged in. They did not want us to reach out and do new but risky things. Avoid risk to ourselves. Also avoid introducing unwanted newness to our people, our world." As she spoke, she was thrumming softly. "We have carefully but thoroughly excluded violence from our culture. And death also."

"Yet your crewmembers were killed."

"Yes, unbearably traumatic." Her thrumming became a raspy gurgle. "Tore me apart inside. My two minds experience a vast inner conflict. I can speak about it calmly with you, but inside I rage: why did I not also die? I could not react fully to their deaths because I was injured. As I recover from injuries, their deaths are very difficult for me to contemplate."

"I am so sorry that I did not have the opportunity to meet your fellow adventurers," I said with a lump in my throat.

She immediately went philosophical again. "I see that this is the price of adventure. Do we choose to pay it?" She was silent for a time, but with flashing skin patches. The dark maroon was gone.

"I have lived the tragedy of choosing, of risking, of risking even my life, for the chance at passion. We risked all, we risked losing it all. We did lose it all. They died; I almost died. I lost my friends, my clan, my world. But exercising real choice is what matters. Even if we lose it all, it doesn't matter, because it was our choice. Not forced on us. Having survived, I now choose to be here with you. To sing with you. For as long as I may live." Her skin patches were once again a bright pink.

16. What Does the Caged Bird Sing?

I was worried that Clay and Doc wouldn't show up for dinner, but there they came. In one car. Laughing and joking.

They climbed out, slamming the car doors, and walked up to the rear entrance where I was waiting. "We figured you didn't give a hoot for either of us, so we might as well be friends," said Clay with a dig.

"Aw, that hurts, guys. You are my two best friends. Except for Breadbox, of course. But no matter, I'll still give you some of this nice red. It's been breathing a while."

What was I thinking? This evening was definitely going to take more than one bottle.

"I need to run something by you guys," I said as I shepherded them around to my front deck.

We all flopped on our favorite chairs on my deck, glasses of Carmenere in hand.

"Shoot. We're all ears."

"I don't know where to start. I had an unexpected experience when I sang in Berkeley two nights ago."

They sat silently, waiting for me to say something significant.

"As I think you know, I haven't felt very excited about my singing career lately. When Breadbox showed up, I considered retiring to focus on her. But I keep getting pulled back into these gigs. I play my old standards, which people still like well enough, but I'm feeling bored with them."

"Why don't you write and sing new stuff?" asked Clay.

"That's just the thing. I haven't written anything decent in a long time. Well, not anything I'm willing to play in public. I'm very insecure about my music. I don't know how people receive it."

"This is news to me," Clay continued. "You seem like one of the most out there, self-assured people I've ever met. I'm envious of your ability to relate to anybody."

"Playing the extravert to cover the inner introvert. That's me. And especially with my music."

"You're not making any sense, woman." Clay said with a frown. "You've long been a successful singer. You have lots of fans. And you're good. I contrast you to that talentless teenybopper you shared the stage with at Locos Only recently."

"Even I listened to some of your music," added Doc, the lover of opera. "I liked it. You're much better than I thought."

"Thanks, I appreciate that."

"Okay. Go on. What is it you're wanting to tell us? And can I have some more of that wine, please?" Clay held out his glass for me to refill. Doc was sipping more slowly, falling behind.

"Anyway, at Berzerkly, I played this one piece, based on something Breadbox had sung. I played it by accident. People loved it. Took me by surprise."

"Well, are you going to play it for us?" Clay gestured with his hands, thereby slopping his wine a bit, not that this could hurt my deck.

I was very bashful about this. I brought out Gibb, tuned and strummed a bit, then got up the nerve to play it for them. These two big, tough, no-nonsense men, watching me like IRS examiners. I had tears in my eyes when I finished. They were both nodding their heads and smiling.

"I don't get it," said Clay with a shrug. "You have this wonderful music talent, yet you want to keep it under wraps. That's crazy. I loved it. Why aren't you playing this at Locos Only?"

"Hiding your light beneath the bushel," said Doc. "That's from Matthew in the Bible. You have a gift. It's your place in the world to share it."

"I feel like I'm bottled up. Locked in a cage. A cage of my own making."

"Get over it," Clay scolded. "I want to hear that song recorded. I want a promise from you that you will get up and sing it. Next Thursday at Locos."

*   *   *

What did I want? What did I really want to do when I grew up?

This alien had shown up, literally crashed into my life. She risked it all to go for what was most important for her. And here I was, fat and happy (well, do these jeans make me look fat?), and whining about my boring, humdrum life, because I wasn't going for what was most meaningful for me.

Or maybe I was. Maybe what was most important to me was wealth and comfort and avoiding uncomfortable situations. Maybe this cocky, irreverent attitude of mine was just a cover.

Breadbox talked about the tragedy of choosing, of risking it all. Then there's the tragedy of not choosing, of not going for it.

And why not? I was afraid my best songs wouldn't be appreciated; i.e., they wouldn't make me much money. And despite being a performer who prances around on stage in front of thousands of people, I was a private person. I was reluctant to reveal myself.

This was probably why my love life hasn't come close to my fantasies. At the most crucial times, I held back from saying what I felt most deeply, what I really wanted. Holed up in my cage.

17. We Looked at the Stars, and Yearned

"**W**here is your home world?" I asked. Breadbox and I were relaxing on my deck on a clear evening reveling in the riot of stars above. My trials and tribulations with my music career and love life had no impact on my relationship with her. She and I spent more time telling stories, singing to each other and together, and driving around the countryside at night. I had taken her to Santa Rosa, which, while not huge, looked much more urban than the Sonoma coastline.

From my deck, we could see the entire sweep of the heavens. "Can you spot your home star?" I asked.

"Nothing looks familiar to me. We must have traveled a very great distance, even by cosmic standards, because no stars are in the same relative positions. Even the density of stars visible in the sky is different. We spent a lot of time studying star positions, because we wanted to correlate star jumpsites to stars we could see, by eye or by instrument."

One feature was familiar to her—the ribbon of the Milky Way sweeping from south to north. (Her people's name for our galaxy sounded like "sear" to me.) She was puzzled, though, because it seemed fainter here. Did this mean her world was closer to the center of the galaxy, and thus the Milky Way looked brighter in her sky?

"Perhaps my device, my wand, which you call Wanda, can help us answer our questions." She held it up toward the sky with two tentacles.

By checking online for the position of constellations and stars, I was able to spot the Andromeda Galaxy in the sky. I was pretty proud of myself for being able to figure this out, since my astronomy skills didn't even reach the level of good astrological readings. But I found it! And I'd never before noticed it, despite all the evenings I had spent sitting on my deck stargazing. On a clear moonless night like this it appeared as an oval smudge of dim light larger than the full moon.

We had no units in common—"light year" meant nothing to her, or to Wanda, because it relates to the length of our year. They hadn't been here a year. At first I was at a loss how to convey this concept, but then I had an aha! "Light day! Wanda knows how long our day is, and knows the speed of light. A light year is 365 light days." I was impressed with myself for figuring this out.

Wanda beeped to Breadbox, who said, "Wanda understands this, and will take measurements of stars and galaxies until it can calculate distances to parts of the galaxy we recognize. But I must leave it exposed so it can observe the night sky."

Interesting. Wanda translates for Breadbox, and now Breadbox translated for Wanda.

Here I learned something new about Wanda. Its instruments could see the stars, and it knew astronomy. It made several observations: The position of Andromeda in relation to the swath of the Milky Way seemed to indicate that we were on the same side of our galaxy as Breadbox's world. At her home, Andromeda appeared closer to The Milky Way in the sky, suggesting that Breadbox's world was deeper into the disk of our galaxy. Using all of this, Wanda calculated that Earth was further from the center of the Milky Way, and closer to the edge of the disk.

Hearing this, Breadbox responded, "Yes, we chose worlds to jump to that were farther away from the galaxy center, because we knew they lay beyond the Confederation."

"From all that you have told me, your world seems like mine in many ways."

"If it were not, I could not be alive here. I could not breathe your air, or see and hear you. As different as you and I are, it is surprising how similar our eyesight and hearing are."

"Are most worlds around other stars like this one?"

"No, very rare. But we seek out such worlds. As we approached your world, we spotted the other planets circling your sun. Large, cold gas worlds. Cold, stony worlds. Small, hot worlds close to your star. Most worlds are like those.

"We sought worlds with the signatures of water and oxygen and organic substances, circling a stable reddish or yellow star. Most such worlds have life, but not beings that build cities and look to the stars.

"It is very dark here where you live, but as we approached your world, we noticed how brightly lit it is on the night side. Much more so than ours. Our world looks dim from above. We use dimmer lights than you do, even in our cities. Yours is more like the main world of the Confederation, called Everbright. Called that because the lights are always on brightly in the cities, and the world is covered by cities."

"Yes, all our cities spew light into the night sky. Makes it hard to view stars. Here on the coast, the stars are often obscured by clouds or fog blowing in from the ocean. But on a warm, clear night like tonight, the sky is glorious."

"On many worlds like yours, the gases in the sky make it hard to see the stars. Even if there are world races that have tools and build cities, they have little connection with the sky.

"My people, even from the earliest days when we emerged from the marshes, always turned our eyes toward the stars. And yearned. In recent times, it seems people have forgotten the heavens, and cast their eyes downward to everyday affairs.

"But not my friends and I. We always looked at the stars in the sky, and wondered. And yearned. Then something magnificent happened for us."

18. The Wilding

"**B**readbox, you were the singer and storyteller of your team, you told me. I would like to hear more about your other crewmembers, if you are willing to talk about them. Who were they? How did all of you come together?"

"I told you earlier why young females and young males could make the best team. She is creative and inventive, he—the organizer and engineer. In recent times, these teams are discouraged, because they are considered too adventurous.

"This is exactly what happened with us—even more so, because two females and a male came together. We three had complementary skills, and we urged each other to take an adventurous path. A forbidden path."

"I want to hear about this," I assured her. "Please let me refill my glass."

"I will gladly tell you, because I am the story teller. On our team, my role was artist, singer, and storyteller. I chronicled and interpreted everything we did."

"I love the name Breadbox you have bestowed upon me, but my home name is Bvar-nala-nga. My dearest friends call me Nala."

"Our second crew member, Analala-noa, also female, was the inventor. Best friends called her Alala. She was the one that discovered the metallic crystal and figured out what it was."

"The third member of our team, Rleza-novan-nga was male—an engineer. He was called Novan. He built all the equipment and adapted the ancient codes contained in the crystal to modern navigation and jump equipment. He alone outfitted the vessel for our journey. He started with a small pleasure craft and transformed it into a star-jumping explorer."

"Alala was our captain; she laid out the itinerary; Novan was the navigator, translating Alala's guidance into effective jumps across space."

"Alala was also our creative problem solver. We relied on her to figure a way out of jams."

"How did the three of you first come together?" I asked.

"We three met on a Wilding. This is a period of craziness for young females and males just before their time of Choosing."

To me, as she described it, the Wilding sounded like a combination of Spring Break and Carnival before Lent. But it went on for much longer.

Besides the normal craziness of the Wilding, all three were rebelling against the life channels they were being forced into. So they became good friends—and conspirators.

"Alala, in her 'young woman's' research and exploring phase, had discovered the metallic crystal in a trinket shop."

"How did she find it? Does your world have little shops like ours?"

"She didn't find it on our world, but while she was visiting a central world of the Confederation. In the old cities of these worlds one can discover artifacts from so many different worlds. Many small items. Often one cannot determine what their purpose was. Most are useless, though rare finds are sometimes made. But they are easy to overlook."

"Why was she looking in such shops?"

"She sought scraps or fragments containing archaic modes of notation. Ancient and forgotten symbols. That was her area of study.

"Since most world races in the Confederation are vertical bipeds like you, items in shops are displayed for their viewing convenience. My people, the Fofonoloy, are horizontal and lower to the ground. Alala had to stand on her hindmost footpads to see the goods, and her eyes were much closer to them. Thus she could see details often missed by others."

"Was she looking for something in particular?"

"She sought flat, incised pieces with symbolic information, designed to retain legibility much longer than any energy-driven piece can. They may be metallic or glass.

"When she found the piece, she told us she knew instantly that it was something very old and special. She had studied archaic modes of notation. She recognized the patterns of incision to be the notation patterns of an ancient, almost mythological, progenitor race—far older than the Fofonoloy of our world. Older even than the oldest oki races of the Confederation. An oki race had built an empire spanning much of this part of the galaxy long before the Confederation came into existence."

"But the patterns were untranslatable—by her or anybody else. They combined elements of both numerical data and storytelling description. As if it were a story about numbers. It looked to Alala like logical symbols constructed of bits of story."

I thought of our DNA, but instead of the standard ACGT protein building blocks (yes, I looked it up), the genes would be built of tiny images of the person whose DNA it was.

At this point I went down to my house and retrieved the amulet from my hidey-hole to show to Breadbox. I noticed I had been reluctant to reveal it to her. Not sure why. Maybe afraid she would take it and somehow fly away home. When she saw it, she shrank away at first, then leaned forward to look closely. "Yes, this is the crystal that Alala found. We put it on this chain to be able to retrieve it from the opening in the vessel's control panel."

"I have called it an amulet, which means a stone with mystical powers to protect you."

"You are very good at naming. Yes, it does have mysterious powers, but instead of protecting us, it got us in trouble. But I too will call it the amulet."

She was clearly fascinated—like a Hobbit seeing the One Ring in Lord of the Rings. But she made no move to take it from me, or even to touch it. She extended one eyestalk very close, as if examining the amulet with a magnifying glass.

Good idea, I thought. So I dashed back to my house, got my large magnifier and a bright lamp, so I could see these things she was describing.

When I got back, I placed the amulet and chain on the corner of her gurney, and we both hunched over it— Breadbox with her two eyestalks held close together, and me with my big glass—as if examining the Hope Diamond, or more likely, the Rosetta Stone.

With the glass, I could clearly see clusters of repeating symbols with slight variations. Breadbox narrated what her partner Alala had done.

"Using her devices, she isolated each cluster, and then ran a series of these clusters through the language translator, a task for which it had not been designed.

"She was delighted to discover that each cluster evoked a tiny song from the translator. When she fed in a whole series of them, it created a harmony—giant chords. The more clusters she fed in, the more complex and beautiful the harmony.

"But she had no idea what it signified."

At this point, Breadbox went into her storyteller mode, recreating what had transpired on that far away planet, in song and lyrical prose.

*   *   *

My partner Alala brought the amulet and her translated music to the Wilding and shared it with us, her new trusted friends. Late one night we were sitting on a small knoll beneath the stars, listening once again to this eerie, mysterious music.

I said to my friends Alala and Novan, "It sounds like the song of the Universe."

"What song would the Universe sing that one would go to the trouble to encapsulate in a small metallic crystal?" asked Novan.

"Perhaps it sings a picture of the Universe," responded Alala. "Or our galaxy. Or part of our galaxy—our surrounding star neighborhood."

"Why did the ancients want a picture of the stars when all they had to do was look up at night to see them in all their glory?" I mused.

"Perhaps it matches the song-image of the star with information about that star," said Novan. "But what kind of information?"

"Where they are? Their coordinates? How to get to them?" I guessed.

We saw the truth of this hit my friend Alala. "That's exactly right!

That's what it is! This is a songstory of the stars, describing how to jump to them."

"But what stars?" I wanted to know.

"Perhaps the ones we see in the sky right now." Alala pressed on. "The amulet contains the data needed to jump from star to star. Of course, not the stars themselves, but the worlds surrounding them."

"There were so many songs you played for us," I exclaimed. "How many worlds then?"

"Yes, thousands," Alala said excitedly. "And I only examined a tiny fraction of the crystal."

"I wonder if it includes our home world?" I asked the question all were thinking.

We had figured out what it must be, but had no way to confirm it. That would be Novan's job.

I asked, "What if it does contain jump codes to unknown worlds not visited for untold years? Are we going to visit them? Or will we turn this over to the keepers of knowledge, to once again be hidden and suppressed?"

"The question answers itself," said Alala. "It would be sacrilege against the ancient inner spirit of our people to allow this not to be used."

"If it is to be done, we three must do it," intoned Novan.

*   *   *

Breadbox explained that for these three, the crazy times of the Wilding completely disappeared—but their collaboration, one might say conspiracy, was born. It took far more than a year, during which they kept putting off their Choices.

Novan found a well-used pleasure yacht that wealthy clan members had long used to jump to vacation worlds around their confederation. As Alala worked out the mathematics of the song codes contained in the crystal, Novan adapted navigational equipment to be able to read this entirely new form of communication data.

When Alala had entered a significant portion of the song codes into the display field of her visualizing instruments, they made a momentous discovery. The song codes were arranged physically within the crystal in the same relationships as the stars in the heavens.

Breadbox continued her narrative and Wanda translated:

*   *   *

We were excited to discover that the crystal was a miniature three-dimensional model of the galaxy—or at least a good part of it. We could clearly discern its spiral arm structure. We quickly identified known star clusters. This allowed us to pinpoint the code for our own star. If we knew where we were starting from, we could figure out where we wanted to go.

Alala matched up song codes with known jumpsite codes to the familiar worlds of our Confederation. But the codes of the crystal extended far beyond, to stars outside the Confederation. The realization was overwhelming. There were new worlds out there to discover, and we had the means to get there!

Now, we had no idea what the worlds that lay beyond the known boundaries would be like. But by closely comparing the ancient codes to the Confederation's codes, we saw that the song codes were generally for the kind of water-oxygen worlds we would want to travel to.

Did we dare jump to a known world using the new jump codes? A frightening prospect. Instead, Novan fashioned a few small robot devices to make the jump—hopefully unnoticed—then send back information to us. This worked the very first time! The eons-old jumpsite we selected was still functioning.

Next we jumped a small robot device to a world outside the known circle of the Confederation and awaited its return signal. The jumpsite functioned well, the signal came back, but there was no world in the vicinity. The robot's instruments picked up a large gas giant in an orbit farther out, but no planet in the path of this device.

On the third try, we were able to pick up readings from a world of the right size and mass, but covered with exceedingly cold clouds. Not an appealing target. Things change in the cosmos, given long- enough time periods. But amazingly, the jumpsites were still functional.

Alala then proposed that we choose a target world to jump to, then send the small robot device to make sure a desirable world was there, and that there were no huge threats or hazards.

Then Novan, the practical one, asked, 'Why don't we send more sophisticated robot vessels to explore for us, rather than risk ourselves?'"

A long silence ensued, but then Alala and I responded in unison, 'Because we want to go!' Novan had no choice but to agree.

*　　*　　*

Breadbox paused in her delivery to allow Wanda to catch up with the translation. "That is how three untested youths made the commitment to leap into a void that none from our civilization had ever attempted before."

"You three made awesome discoveries that none of your Elders had done. In deciphering the stone, in mathematics, in guidance devices for the spaceship. And made them work. If all your people are this inventive . . . I glimpse why some drew back from the potential of your people's capacity for invention and adventure."

"Yes, I now see this also," said Breadbox. "Was this the wisdom of our Elders? They thought so. Judging by the results, they were correct."

I disagreed. "If you three had succeeded in your quest, you could have changed the direction of history in this galaxy."

"Not our intention," she said. "We just wanted an adventure. Better that we failed."

"But you didn't. Here you are. You may still succeed in doing this." I paused before voicing a hidden thought. "I would love to go with you back to the stars."

She drew back from me a bit when I said that, then said, "I would much rather stay and sing stories with you." Her skin patches flashed mauve and violet. "We should destroy this amulet."

I picked it up, clasped it in my hand, then put it in my pocket. I didn't want it destroyed. Like the One Ring of Power.

Was I being like Frodo or Gollum? Or Sauron?

19. I Reek Havoc

"Agate, my best friend, I want to go with you when you sing."
Breadbox could not be dissuaded. She had been insisting that I take her along, so she could see what I do in front of an audience. She had refused her Choice to become the singer for her clan, and now she was urging me to own up to my "choice" to be a singer—despite all the cynical things I've said about singing for a living.

I wanted to please her. In truth, I wanted her to be my accompanist at a concert. Wow! Would that ever be a boost to my career! Variety would scream, "Fading rock star's career boosted by funny-looking alien backup singer."

On the other hand, I was not nearly ready to spring her on the world and have to explain everything. And draw attention to my secretly stashed spaceship.

Now that I was again taking Morty's calls, the gig spigot had been turned on. Morty lined me up a gig at a music festival in Point Arena, a ways north up Highway 1. This was an easy one. Local event, informal venue. Outside in a natural amphitheater. I would be just one of a number of bands and singers. Pay was so-so but it was like going to a neighborhood party.

Breadbox had recognized Morty's voice on the speakerphone, understood what he said (with Wanda's help), and begged me to bring her along. She danced around like a kid who hears the ice cream truck coming up the street.

What a crazy idea. I had to recruit Clay. First, because I needed his pickup truck to haul my gear, which he had done for me more than once. Also, I would need him to babysit Breadbox while I was on stage.

You know, guys let themselves be talked into anything by a woman!

Clay actually got into it. "How can we make it so that Breadbox can enjoy the concert and watch you sing? And me too. I want to hear you sing. I won't even have to buy a ticket, will I?

I replied, in crazy mode, "Maybe we could bring her on stage as a piece of equipment? Could we disguise her as an amp?"

Clay played along. "She'd want to sing along with you! Put her in a costume of some sort."

I giggled, "I can see the headline. 'Alien in bear suit causes ruckus at local music festival.'"

"Hmmm, maybe not," said Clay. "But if we get there early and get a good parking spot up at the top of the hill, Breadbox and I can watch and hear you from the back of the truck. I'll rig up a little tent over the truck bed to conceal her from prying eyes."

This seemed like a crazy plan, especially if my goal was to avoid risking public exposure to my favorite secret alien. But being crazy didn't always stop me. I'm not sure: is that a good thing or a bad thing in my life?

Clay drove; Breadbox sat on the console between us, just like Buddy used to do. Brought back pangs of loss. How would he have responded to Breadbox, I wondered? And vice versa. Clearly he was an intelligent being. Would she consider him an oki? A semi-oki like Farmer Jed's cat? Would Wanda have been able to translate his "dog talk" like she did with the crows?

Between my place and Point Arena, Highway 1 goes along some of the most gorgeous ocean cliffs in the world, with the Pacific just a hundred-yard plunge down to our left. But very twisty and turny. And guess what. Breadbox got carsick! Who knew? All the curves did her in. Just like Buddy. Thank goodness she didn't upchuck; she just felt really bad and moaned and twitched. Clay drove even slower, which aggravated all the giant Winnebagos looming behind us.

Point Arena is a tiny town on the Mendocino coast that has seen logging and fishing and farming, and still retains some of the left-over hippie vibe from a generation or so ago. Probably because it's hard to get to, it has been less gentrified by upscale folks fleeing the city. A perfect place for an informal country music festival with rock, blues, reggae, and other genres.

Sure enough, they had parking reserved for the performers on the hill beside the natural amphitheater. It was perfect. Clay parked his pickup truck with the tailgate toward the stage. Breadbox was perched there, in the bed of the truck. Clay draped a tarp over the frame above his truck bed, and then wrapped Breadbox in a blanket with her eyestalks sticking up, so she could see and hear everything, and hopefully not be seen.

I was glad to see, looking at the stage setup, that I wouldn't need my own amp or mike, or anything else but my guitar.

I gave Breadbox instructions like you would a six-year old kid. "Now stay here. You will be able to see me down there on that platform. And hear me sing. There will be some other singers also. Stay wrapped up. Do what Uncle Clay asks you to." Hoping she understood—and assented—I tromped down the hill, carrying Gibb.

This small valley, with its gently sloping sides, made a perfect amphitheater during the dry season. They put a platform over the bottom end, and people spread out their blankets and folding chairs all over the hillside. Attire ranged from overalls and boots, to shorts and flip-flops, to high-ticket jeans and leather jackets. Many mellowed out with the local weed, and the smoke drifted up toward the parking lot. Could Breadbox get a second-hand high, I wondered?

I was Number 3 on the bill, after Eddy Backwater, who does country, and Dawgbreath, a local rock group. I huddled just off stage where I could watch how they did.

Eddy Backwater was the warmup. He and I have a history. He pretends like I've got the hots for him. Not. Au contraire! It's a love/hate relationship. He loves me, I hate him. No, that's not true. He's okay.

He bounced up onto the stage holding his Stratocaster like an axe. Skinny, scruffy, unshaven, looked one step up from homeless. He was wearing his trademark "I Reek Havoc" tee shirt, ten-gallon hat, and platform cowboy boots to make him look taller. He does his East Texas drawl pretty good, but I know he's actually from Brooklyn.

He's not a great musician, but he gets the crowd involved. "It's good to be back here where I feel right at home. Hey, look, I got a new tat across my shoulders." He pulled up his tee shirt to reveal a large tattoo, from shoulder to shoulder, of a sexy brunette in a bikini draped across a giant martini glass. "Want to get a picture of this? Hold up your cellphones, everybody, and get a shot of this. Hold 'em high. Hold 'em high."

He turned around suddenly and pointed at the audience. "Aha, just as I suspected. Not a shaved armpit in the entire crowd—men or women. That's why I feel so at home here on the Mendocino coast." They groaned or roared with laughter.

Eddy did a few of his standards about lost love and heartbreak and a

Eddy Backwater

81

hound dog that won't hunt, telling corny stories between each one. Then sat down to laughter and applause.

Dawgbreath is best at oldies but goodies. That's fine—most of the people here are oldies. They're looking for goodies to sing along with.

My playlist was like that also. I wasn't getting paid enough to arrange any new stuff. So I just put together a few of my old standards.

When my turn came, I climbed up onto the stage, held my guitar, looked out at the audience. I looked above them, at the surrounding hills, at the crescent moon in the darkening sky, just after the sun had set. What an absolutely gorgeous fall evening it was!

This had a strange effect on me. For a moment, standing in front of all these people waiting expectantly for me to sing, I had this weird reaction. I couldn't remember—what was I here for? What am I supposed to do for these people? What were they paying for? Of course I knew that a lot of them hadn't paid anything—they just snuck in from the woods. But even then, if they go to the effort to sneak in, there's something they want. What do they want?

They wanted communion. They wanted to connect. Not just with each other right then, but with their own selves over their lifetimes. They were there to reconnect with their younger, passionate, all-things-are-possible selves. The passion of the twenty-something rekindled in the fifty-something spirit. Music can do that.

I was the secular priestess. Leading the ceremony of reconnection. Singing the words that allow them to connect with me and with each other—and with themselves.

And up in a truck that was parked looking down over this congregation was this alien being who had travelled who knows how far, and was here in Point Arena, California, to hear me sing on this beautiful summer evening.

"Ladies and gentlemen, I am honored to be here with you tonight. I am going to sing a couple of my pieces that you all know. You might know them better than me. I want you to sing along, because, who knows, I might forget some of the words, and you can help me out."

When I perform, I look out over the audience, focusing on people toward the back. I avoid looking at people sitting right in front, because the eye connection can throw me off. What are they thinking about me, I wonder.

Their eyes can be so open, like they're drinking in the music. Their souls are exposed. And it's due to my music. It's hard for me to share that connection with them, especially when I'm feeling just ho-hum about what I'm singing.

But that night, under the spell of what I'd just experienced, I dared to look them in the eyes, including folks right in the front row. It did throw me off, and I dropped a line, but the audience kept singing and clapping, and carried the tune. I got through it, and I loved it.

By the time I finished three songs, tears were streaming down my face. "Thank you, thank you. My heartfelt thanks to you. You're a wonderful audience."

Then I did it—I don't know why. Despite what I'd said about not doing any new stuff, I heard my inner crazy woman saying, "I'll finish with a new piece I've been working on, to see how you like it. I wouldn't dare play this most places, but here on the coast among my own people, on a beautiful evening, where the whole broad cosmos may be watching and listening—I might just dare it.

"You may not like it. Doesn't matter. I'm singing it for myself."

I played the melody I had first performed at Berzerkly. I had worked on it some, and played it for Breadbox, and for Clay and Doc. And Joel. It was originally her melody. Tonight it was just Gibb and my wordless vocalizing as counterpoint to the guitar.

That's when I heard Breadbox singing along, clear as an organ chord, up on the hill where Clay was parked. Ay yi yi! Could people hear her over the amplified music?

When I was finished, the audience went wild. I got a standing ovation. People shouted "Encore, encore!"

The emcee came on stage to thank me, and said, "Sorry, we can't do an encore just now. We have to honor the remaining groups. Right now, we'll take a short break. Back in twenty with Flasher and their new hit, Grrrr!" I took a bow, jumped off the stage, and sprinted up the hill toward the truck.

*   *   *

Meanwhile, up in the parking lot…. (Clay recounted this to me later.)

When Breadbox heard me sing this familiar melody, she rose up in the back of Clay's truck, threw off her concealing blanket, and sang out in her various voices, singing along with me in a wonderful duet. Probably not audible to the crowd over the amplified music, but plainly so to those close by. This did not go unnoticed by a young kid with his mother.

"Mom! There's a strange animal in that pickup. Look! It's a giant bug. No, I think it's an ET!"

"Jack Jr., did you just spit on the ground? What if everybody did that?"

"Everybody, Mom? Everybody in the world? It would make a mountain of spit ten stories high that would ooze and gurgle and run down the creek, yucky and putrid and full of all kinds of germs." He tugged her hand. "Mom, come look at the alien monster. Maybe it's from Mars."

"Your imagination will be your ruin, young man."

"It's on the back of that truck with that tall man, singing."

"Don't point. Don't stare at people. It's rude. Now come on. I'll buy you a sno-cone."

Jack Jr. stared back over his shoulder as his mom dragged him away.

83

Eddy Backwater, up in the parking area to sneak a toke, edged closer, to see this so-called ET.

Eddy's first thought was "This is great music; where's Selena? Does she have a speaker in her truck? It's kind of like karaoke. Or maybe it's malfunctioning recording equipment." Then he caught a glimpse of this strange being as Clay frantically tried to wrap up Breadbox in a blanket.

Eddy was on it. "What the hell do you have there, man? Say, aren't you Selena's boyfriend? What the hey?" He took out his phone and shot a snippet of video before Clay could even answer.

Clay is a big guy, and he threw Eddy a look that could catch somebody's hair on fire. Eddy backed off fast. "Hey, I'm skedaddling!"

*   *   *

Eddy disappeared between two cars just as I arrived, panting. "Omigod, Clay. I heard her singing!"

"Oh, yeah, she sang along, all right. Not just with you, but with the other performers. Even that Eddy Backwater. Who, by the way, heard her, came right up to the truck, and snapped a photo.

"I got to say, Selena, I was—shall we say—nonplused. How could I keep her from being noticed by people wandering around? I tried to talk with her, and asked her to sing quietly. But maybe she—and her translating tube—aren't familiar with my voice. They ignored me. So I got in the back of the truck with her and sang along. Tried to mask her sound with my squeaky tenor."

Anyway, Clay was more than ready to go. So I didn't even get to stay to the end and hear the headliners.

Breadbox was jubilant! All the way home, she sang these riffs off my melodies and made entirely new songs out of them. And I didn't even record it.

But pesky Eddy had photos of her. How soon would we see that on the internet?

20. How to Jump Between Stars

Breadbox wanted to see the bright lights. I took her on a nighttime road trip through the countryside, down the 101 freeway, almost to the Golden Gate Bridge. We turned off and drove up the steep hill of the Marin Headlands. From there, we looked down over the top of the Golden Gate Bridge and marveled at the bright lights of San Francisco across the bay—like a fairyland city suspended above the dark water. We could see the distant ascending lights of the aircraft taking off from the San Francisco airport, south of the city.

"Are those vessels departing for other worlds?" she wanted to know.

"No, my people travel only to other parts of this world. We are mainly limited to this planet, except for some probes sent to other parts of our star's system." I was a bit embarrassed to admit that we are such primitives! "We travel to other worlds around our star, such as the moon you see in our sky. But not to other stars. And most of our space vessels contain only instruments, not living beings."

"We discussed sending a robot," she said. "This would have been safer. But Alala and I urged Novan to go in person, so he agreed. We wanted to see the new worlds for ourselves."

"In that way, your people and mine are very similar. We also love to explore in person. But it is very costly."

"Not 'my people,' only we three," she reminded me. "Forbidden for others. And it was also costly to us."

"But your people travel to other worlds within the Confederation." She had told me about these trips.

"True, they do. They stay sealed up inside the vessel. Close the hatch on one end of the journey. Go into stasis. Awaken in time to open the hatch on the other end. People are hardly aware they are traveling. But during our explorations, we three stayed awake and alert every moment, constantly watching. The wonder of everything!"

"Yes, I get that," I nodded agreement. "Whenever I travel by aircraft, I always sit next to the window so I can watch the clouds, and the countryside below.

"Tell me more about how you accomplished this travel," I requested.

"Earlier you asked me where my world lies, and we could not explain; we did not know. Wanda has now completed observations and calculations." She held Wanda apart from her to indicate that Wanda was speaking for herself, not translating Breadbox.

"After conducting observations of the night sky over several nights, interrupted by clouds, Wanda has reached a conclusion," Wanda explained in her tour director voice.

"There is a cluster of stars about 35% of the way around our galaxy, and closer to the center, that is expanding in a predictable way. It is more distant than our world, but in the same general direction. It is quite prominent in the night sky of our world. Wanda has been able to locate it in your sky by using maximum magnification. By comparing its apparent size here and on our world, Wanda can estimate its distance. By knowing its rate of expansion, and knowing that it was smaller when the light you see was created, Wanda can estimate even more closely. By entering data on the likely direction of our home star, and then converting to your units of distance, Wanda estimates that our star lies at a distance of 3,800 to 4,700 of your light years."

It took a minute for this to soak in. "You are saying that you and your crew traveled from your world to ours—a distance that it takes light about 4,000 of our years to travel—in a very short time?"

"But of course we used the star jump. We didn't actually travel all that distance."

"Wait. I don't understand this," I interrupted. "How does this work? What does it mean to 'jump' between worlds? Our science tells us this is impossible."

"I don't know how it works. Novan was the engineer. He used the wand and the amulet."

Here's how I pieced it together. Now understand, this comes to you via a poet-storyteller to a songwriter-musician, with intercession from a talking metallic tube. So my apologies if you can't grasp the science.

The universe has two (or more?) kinds of space, overlaid. Regular space has all the laws and limits we are familiar with. The other space has different laws. Laws that allow messages, solid things, and even living beings to move from one place to another without passing through the intervening space. Space without distance. Perhaps without time.

It's like on Earth. We can travel on foot only so fast and so far. But suppose there's a telephone where I'm heading. I can just call ahead, seemingly instantaneous. "Telephone space" is completely different from travel-by-foot space. A telephone seems like magic to someone who has never encountered one before. But once you get used to it, you never again send messages by runner.

But initially there are no phones. So somebody first has to travel around on foot to install phones at different locations. They assign each one a number, record it in a directory along with its location, and thereafter you can reach that location merely by calling the number. Now, when you call a phone number, you may have no idea where that phone is located, and maybe you don't care. You only want to connect with the person on the other end.

In a broad swath of our galaxy, probably millions of years ago, robot vessels chugged around between stars at sub-light speed, taking as long as it took, installing jumpsites around stars with interesting planets, like a fleet of cosmic Johnny Appleseeds. Jumpsites were positioned at stable gravitational spots, where they would stay put over eons in relation to the worlds they wanted to visit. Thereafter, vessels could get there by jumping through the other plane of space —the one with no time or distance—from one star to another.

Unlike the "telephone space" network, with this "space jumpsite" network, you could send not only messages, but also vessels and people and goods.

But in the intervening millions of years the "phone directory" of jumpsites had been lost. Not just the directory, but also the knowledge of those who had created the network and its directory. And even the system of recording the data was lost! Later, when bits of it were found, people didn't recognize it for what it was. Yet the jumpsites themselves still orbited their stars, awaiting a visitor.

Much more recently (tens of thousands of years?), the existing Confederation built up a new network of jumpsites as it expanded. It wasn't as extensive as the prior network; old jumpsites at stars like our Sun lay completely outside the newer network. Also, it was based on a completely different system of communication.

I can't quite grasp the distinction, but it sounds like the more recent Confederation used strings of numbers to identify jumpsites—the way we would do it—whereas the ancient prior civilization had used complex pieces of song. You can see how singing storytellers like the Fofonoloy would be the ones to rediscover them.

Okay. End of lecture on galactic history and science. (But there will be a quiz later!)

I asked Breadbox, "Did you visit other worlds before coming here?"

"Yes, four. But boring. Dark, cold, barren. One covered by sand, one by ice, one by jagged mountains, one by thick forests. We never even landed on any of them. We orbited, recorded data, looked in vain for signs of advanced life, then eventually departed."

"Why choose this world we call Earth? By the way, what is your name for our world?"

"Your world was unknown to our astronomers. It is so distant from our Confederation that your star had never been mapped or given a designation. Thus we didn't know what your world was like before we arrived in your star system.

Breadbox made intricate weaving gestures with two tentacles—the kind that I learned meant what was to come had an emotional charge. "It was a dare. Find a world that is unknown but not barren. One that has some interesting phenomena, and life." She added after a pause, "We viewed this quest as an initiation adventure." Her display of tentacles reminded me of the dance of a many-armed goddess.

"As soon as we jumped into your star system," she went on, "we were quite excited. Your world is so beautiful! We couldn't believe our sensors. There is such a magnificent fountain of coherent radiation patterns filling the space around your world. We had hoped for at most some interesting flora and fauna. Instead, we had discovered by pure chance a world of high technology and advanced beings. Exactly the kind of world we are forbidden to make contact with. Exactly the kind of world we dreamed of finding. Now that we had done so, we were terrified."

"Did you report this back to your home base?" I asked.

"No, we did not, I am sorry to say. Since this was a forbidden voyage, we did not dare. If we had made contact with interesting worlds, if we had proof, then we could have reported back. But instead we had this mishap."

"What would you have done?" I wanted to know.

"I do not know. Your world is so much more than we could have anticipated. If we returned home with artifacts and evidence, we would have been received as heroic explorers by some, even as we were given strong reprimands and punishment by the Elders."

"Can others follow you here?"

"Unlikely," she said. "Alas, no one knows where we went. We kept it secret and concealed any traces of our choices. They would have stopped us. This amulet is unique as far as we know, and we brought it with us. It alone contains the jump codes. We dared not transfer them to other devices, because others would have found them and followed us, and we wanted this to be our voyage of discovery."

"Can you call for help?"

"Oh no, I couldn't do that. I would be too ashamed. I fear their response. The deaths of my two companions weigh upon me."

"But they could come rescue you," I protested.

"They would not do that.""

"Why not?"

"We have broken the greatest taboos. And we failed in our mission."

This was so alien to my way of thinking. Yes, of course, you say, they are aliens! Yet in another part of my noggin, I could totally resonate with her thinking.

"What happened? What caused you to crash?" I asked with some emotion.

"I'm sorry I cannot explain well. I was the youngest and the least formed of our crew. Remember, I was the artist, the poet and singer and chronicler. My role was to sing the song of the journey."

She continued dispassionately, "We may have had the landing protocol set to 'beacon landing' instead of person-controlled visual landing. We were too eager. We should have orbited first. The device sought a beacon to lock onto, to cede control so it could guide us in. When there was no beacon, of course, we were coming in too low, too fast. The vessel hit the atmosphere like a wall, turned, tumbled, broke apart." After a pause, she continued, "We tried to crash in the sea so no remains of us would be found."

I could think of nothing to say to this. We sat in silence for a time, watching the beautiful lights of the city, then sang a quiet song together.

21. Shaggy Dog Story

On the way back, I needed to go by a store, and I stopped at a city park in San Rafael to use the facility. This late in the evening it looked deserted. The restrooms were up against a wooded hill. Breadbox was fascinated by the playground equipment. There's a spaceship toy for kids to climb on, and she had to check that out. Then she wanted to crawl through the tunnel—like a big section of culvert. I avoided even thinking about her wanting to try the swings. Yikes, how would we do that?

When I used the restroom, I was curious about the extension cord plugged into the outlet that was trailing into the shrubbery behind it.

I should have known! A shaggy guy came ambling out of the bushes. "Hey! Don't unplug my cord! Got the TV connected to that!"

After a momentary fear of being accosted, I recovered and made nice. "Sounds like you got pretty fancy digs here! What kind of reception do you get?"

"Well, it's not too bad here as long as I don't get hassled! The rent is right. TV don't matter; I got DVDs." He was pretty proud of himself. "Say, what kind of dog is that you've got over there? I was watching it run around!"

"Yeah… it's one of those… shaggy… afghan… sheep hounds! It's a rescue animal. I want to get it acclimated out here when other people are not around. So, don't get too close, okay?" Strike 2!

Next I stopped at the 7 11 to pick up some half-and-half for the morning. Man, late at night that place is like the Star Wars Bar! I figured Breadbox would fit right in, but I implored her to stay in the back of the Jeep, covered up. But not quite covered up enough, because she attracted the attention of a woman sitting on the curb who might already have been communing with beings from outer space, from the way she looked.

Just as I came out of the store, she was edging up close, poking at Breadbox with a stick. I tried to get between her and the Jeep, and she said, "Sheeeeyit! What you got under that blanket, girl?"

"Hey hey, calm down! Halloween's coming up. It's for my kid's costume. Don't tell anybody, okay?"

All right. Three close scrapes. When are we going to go public? I saw I had to get together with my posse and talk about how to bring my friend out of the closet.

And of course, that means laying the whole story out there for the world. I can't keep this a secret forever. I got the willies! Bad.

22. Slick Slim's Slither Inn

It was Morty calling. I was tempted not to take his call. "Sel, I hate doing this to you, but I've got another cancellation. Good club, good money, and they want somebody of top quality. Nice gig for you. Club Xanadu in Venice.

"Oh yeah, I've done that place. Young crowd, but also lots of tourists. They still like my music?"

"They'll like it well enough," he said, with just a hint of bluster. "You just got to come down and sing it. They had a cancellation, and they want you to be the headliner."

"When?"

"This Saturday." Oy. That means I have to go through the babysitter hassle again. Better recruit Clay this time.

"Money plus all costs, right? I don't want to stay in that dump they put me in last time."

"No, no, this time it's one of the big hotels down by LAX."

*　　*　　*

Xanadu is a decent club in Venice just south of Santa Monica, a street away from the beach. Originally it was a movie theatre, so it has a big floor space. I would rather have been playing next door at Slick Slim's Slither Inn—rowdy, down and dirty, noisy and enthusiastic. But the money was good, and Morty had wangled a nice room at the Marriott.

As I walked up to the entrance of Xanadu, an icy shock of fear ran up my spine. The marquee of Slick Slim's announced Eddy Backwater as the number-two act. I'd been avoiding him ever since his encounter with Breadbox and Clay at Point Arena.

But inside, the crowd energized me, and I forgot about Eddy. I started off with my standards and soon had people clapping along. I did a couple of irreverent and funny ones, just to loosen up the crowd. First . . .

> *Would you take a true love lie detector*
> *to prove your love to me?*

92

Next . . .

I'm playing with you
the game of love
and I'm losing every match.

Then a bit of poignancy.

Pretending I'm still in love with you
so I'll have someone to come home to.
Faux love is much much better than no love.

I continued with a rousing rendition of *I Got Sugar For Ya Baby* and then went into *Cotton Candy Lovin'*. God, how they ate it up.

*   *   *

At my break, I snuck out to the back alley to catch some fresh air. No such luck. The smell of pot was overpowering. There was Eddy smoking a doobie, wearing a ratty tee shirt that said "My Other Car Is a John Deere."

He spotted me and sidled right over. "Sel, good to see ya. It's been awhile." He did reek. I could get a second-hand high just standing next to him.

"Y'know, I can keep a secret," he snickered.

"Oh yeah? What secret is that?"

"I can keep a secret about that strange thing in the back of your boyfriend's truck at Point Arena."

"What do you think he had in the truck? Just my amp and guitar."

"Some strange-looking beast. Kind of singing along with you. The kid that was hanging around said it was an ET."

"Eddy, I don't know what you saw. But a stoned-out guy like you won't have much cred when you start talking about aliens."

"Well, you just might be right about that. Lucky for me I snapped a snippet of video with this here phone, which does pretty good in low light."

He held up his phone so I could see. There was Breadbox, unmistakable, singing away, while Clay frantically tried to throw a blanket over her head.

I stood mute. Oh god, here it comes. I could just see this spread across every social media site. I knew I shouldn't have taken her up there.

"I can keep a secret, but I have a price."

"Oh no, here comes the blackmail demand. What do you want? Money or sex?"

"Nothing like that, though I'm sure you're getting paid better'n me for these gigs. No, what I want is to be in on that secret. I want to know what you had in that truck bed. Your boyfriend Clay clearly knows. So I should know also. You and I go back a long ways."

"What do you think it was?"

"Well, obviously it was an animal that sings. But strange, I've never heard anything like those tones. It sounded like a little organ come to life."

"It wasn't alive. Why would you think that?"

"Oh yes! Eyes. Eyes on eyestalks. Like a giant snail. Waving around, in time with the music."

"And I know what you're planning to do," he plowed on.

"What's that?" I felt totally caught. Pulled down whatever way he was heading. Couldn't think of any plausible lies. Couldn't even deny it. My brain was in lockdown. The folly of my ways was revealed to me. I had done it against my better judgment because Breadbox insisted. She loved the music, and once she got a taste, she kept wanting more. And could she just sit there silently and listen? Oh no, she was a sing along type o' gal. And now I was about to hear Eddy's outrageous demands.

"Okay, Eddy, lay it on me so I can say no."

He took a big hit, then slowly exhaled, gallantly turning his head aside rather than blowing smoke in my face. "If I had a talking dog, say, the only thing that would make sense would be for me to go on the road with that dog. Right now I play to hundreds. With that dog I'd play to thousands. I'd fill stadiums.

"The way I see it is, you've got some kind of singing animal, an animal that's not known for its singing. So you're breaking it in to take it on the road with you. You and I, we're not getting any younger, and the new acts, as lousy as they are, are pushing us aside. What better way to goose your career?"

What an alluring idea, I thought. But totally impossible. He just didn't know the half of it. And even if I wanted to, I couldn't do this with Breadbox. She was much too fragile.

Eddy took my pause as assent, or at least interest, and pushed on. "So here's what I want. Just two little things. When you play before sold-out houses, I want to be your warmup act. And two, I want a jam session. I want to bring my guitar up to wherever you keep your singing snail and jam to its organ music. Then I'm on your side, and I'll defend your secret to my death."

"Jeez, Eddy, wouldn't you settle for money and sex?" I said with a forced smile that came out as a grimace.

"Not to take anything away from you, Sel, but the money possibility intrigues me most. But only from piggybacking on whatever you've got cooking."

"I don't have anything cooking," I admitted. Perhaps I should. You're familiar with those horns of a dilemma? I was impaled.

"Well, gotta head in for my set. I'll have my people contact your people," he said, as he took the last finger-scorching hit.

"Eddy, get your skinny ass in here," yelled the Slick Slim manager. "You're on in fifteen seconds." Eddy bounded in through the back door. I

94

just had to watch, so I edged up toward the door. Eddy sauntered onto the stage, grabbed his guitar, pulled the mike over to his mouth, and cleared his throat.

"Who are you?" the manager asked me in his 'keep the hell out' voice. Then he actually recognized me! "Selena M! You're headlining at Xanadu, right? Want to check out the good club?"

"Your guy there fascinates me. When he's not repelling me."

"Eddy? He's a crackup. Stand over here out of the way and watch."

"I've got to get back for my second set, but I've got to see his lead-in."

"People over at Xanadu are still waiting for Olivia Newton-John to show up," he chided. "When you're ready to do a real club, have your agent give me a call." He gestured toward Eddy. "Here's our boy."

Eddy grabbed the mike off the stand, tapped it enough to get some good screeching feedback. "Most of you people here don't know me, do you? So I can be anybody I want. Well, who do I want to be? Who am I here tonight? Surely not myself! How about younger, sexier, more hair?" Cheers from the audience. "Naw, way too timid. Hmm, I could be my Virtual Life avatar—cute, alluring, tantalizing!" Laughter. "Neh, too last decade. I got it. Maybe a beast from outer space—angry, slavering, all-powerful, with terrible body odor. Yeah, it has possibilities. But I'd never be able to get a date."

"I'll date you, Eddy!" shouted some mountain mama in the front row.

"I'll tell you who I am. I'm Eddy Backwater, and I'm here to rock this joint tonight, and to offend as many of you as I can."

The audience was wild. People stood up and yelled "Yeee-hawww!! Hurt me, Eddy. Hurt me!"

"Lemme start with a little ditty with an important social message that I learned from those great artists, Homer and Jethro." He strummed a couple of chords, then sang. "I've got tears in my ears from lyin' on my back, in the sack crying tears over you, o my baby . . ."

I turned to go. He was a weasel, a snake, a lousy artist, but he loved what he did. He loved entertaining. And so people loved him. I was jealous. He held a terrible secret over my head and he was demanding a payment.

I steamed out the door, but then had a change of heart. I turned back to the Slick Slim manager. "If I come, I want to sing some new music."

"When I talk to your agent . . . what's his name?"

"Morty."

"Morty, right. He says you'll sing the tried and true standards."

"That's what I'm doing at Xanadu. You want to copy Xanadu? Now you're talking to me, not Morty. And I'm offering to sing some new pieces. Never before recorded. A bit experimental. A new departure for me."

"How experimental? You done these elsewhere?"

"Yes, Berzerkly. Got a roaring ovation."

"I know that place. It's called berserk for a reason."

"I'll mix it up. Oldies and newies. Who knows, your audience might like it."

"What they like is energy. That's what Eddy brings. Energy. Gets 'em fired up. You're a much better singer. Need to grow your energy."

"I hear you."

I need to grow my energy. Indeed. Like if my heart, soul, and passion were in it. It could happen. I headed back into Xanadu. I thought I'd been energizing pretty good tonight.

23. Jam Session

"**B**readbox, my friend, if I brought a few people over to hear us sing together, would that be acceptable with you?" I approached her almost apologetically, but she was immediately excited.

"Your friends have heard us sing before. I am honored to sing for them, if I can sing along with you."

"There's a new friend, whom you have not met, who also plays a guitar. He wants to come also."

"Yes, please," she said with a vibrant shake of her tentacles. "I would love to sing with you—and your friends.

So Eddy got his way. I decided to host a jam session at my house, with music by Breadbox and me, and I invited him. And my buds—Clay, Sheriff Jim, wife Meg, and Doc the vet.

They all came over as the sun was setting, except Eddy, who was very late. Clay had suggested that we all wear our old rock concert tee shirts, and the idea caught on. Doc wore a very ragged Bob Dylan, "The answer is blowing in the wind." Jim wore his faded Grateful Dead shirt, but Meg came in a Hello Kitty tee, just slightly too small. I wore one of my own—a hot pink tank top with "Cotton Candy Lovin'" in sequins.

Clay had an amazing shirt. He'd used a photo of one of Breadbox's sketches and had it printed onto a long-sleeved tee with the caption "Together Stars People." It was a sketch of her and me together, kind of intertwined.

"Oh, I want one!" I exclaimed.

"And I had one made for you," he said as he handed it to me. This earned him a huge hug.

Eddy wore his tattered denim uniform as usual, and brushed off my gripe about being late. "Whaddaya mean? Good parties don't get going till after midnight."

Introductions and small talk. Meg pinned Eddy. "Well, Mr. Drinkwater . . . I'm sorry. I mean, Mr. Blackwater . . ."

"Now ma'am, that's Backwater. Eddy Backwater. And just call me Eddy."

"You married? Any children?" Meg nosed into his life, as she likes to do. No matter, Eddy loved anybody paying attention to him.

"Yeah, two blonds ago, I had a kid. Little girl. Blue-eyed and cute like her mom, not craggy and dark like me. She kinda likes me, but her mom don't."

"Sir, I hope you take good care of your daughter."

"Oh, ma'am, I am a rough, irascible old guy, but I love my little girl. She is the light in my life and keeps me going down the straight and narrow. Who knows where I'd be off to otherwise? You know how some people tithe? Well, I tithe to her. I put money aside every time it comes in. For her future, for her college. So she will get to do whatever she wants. I keep this money out of the clutches of her mom, so that it don't end up on the casino gaming tables."

"Surely you provide child support to her poor mother." Meg sounded ready to pick a fight.

"Oh yes ma'am. The courts have seen to that. All this money set aside is extra. Her mom don't even know about it. And I really can't even tell my girl about it. Until the time comes when she's looking at schools. Then my banker will give her a discreet call."

For a Polish guy from Brooklyn, Eddy does East Texas country boy pretty well. But Meg was suspicious of his Texas cred. "I'm from Texas myself," she said. "Austin. Went to the university. I don't recall Naca . . ."

Eddy squared off with Meg. He didn't want his cover blown. "Well, ma'am, you ain't never heard of Nacogdoches? Why, it's the world capital of compost! Besides being just up the road from the Texas Country Music Hall of Fame. Back on my Pappy's spread, that steer manure is piled so high that the bulldozers can't even make their way to the top of the heap. And the smell? Why, that's why I worked my way out west to seek my fortune in Hollywood. I ain't never made no fortune, sorry to say, but I sure have a hell of a lot of fun singin' with folks. But I never really left my old home. It's still with me. Fact of the matter is, I think I got some stuck to my boots right now."

This was beginning to sound like his stage patter, so I cut in. "Are we going to do some music, or what?"

Just then, there was a knock on the door. Nobody else was expected, so we all tensed up and looked around at each other.

"Can't be the cops," said Doc sardonically. "No dope, no noise, no fights, no underage drinkers. And we already have the sheriff here."

"Unless Eddy blabbed and it's the alien hunters finally caught up with us," said Clay.

"No way, no way," Eddy said defensively. "I know who it is."

I beat Eddy to the door. I don't have one of those peepholes on my front door, so I opened it a crack and peered out into the night. A blast of cool fall wind pushed the door open. There was this short, scruffy guy squinting into my porch light. He avoided my gaze and said nothing, just looked at my feet. Behind him a cart full of luggage or something. Drums! It was drums.

Eddy frowned at me sheepishly. "Hate to spring this on you, but this session needed some percussion, not just guitars. So I brought Carlos. Carlos, come on in. Selena, can Carlos come in?"

I just stood aside, mouth open. Carlos, the little gray man, came in, tugging his cart full of drums and stands. He walked slowly, with an apology in every step. He was even scruffier than Eddy. He didn't talk, but nodded his answers.

"Let's do introductions. Okay, everybody? This is Carlos, my percussionist. Carlos, this is everybody. I've already forgotten your names. Except for Selena here. But you know Selena M., don't you, Carlos?" Carlos nodded shyly.

"Eddy, I'm amazed that you would bring in a stranger, especially on this night. How could you do this?

Carlos finally said something in his soft, meek voice, "I have see my own aliens. No worry about me. No hay problema. I see my own aliens, and I don't talk about them neither."

With his accent, he had to repeat this two and a half times before I could get it.

"And besides," said Eddy, "he's an illegal alien himself. So that's why he ain't talking."

"Eddy, this is exactly why I don't trust you. First thing you do is blab your friend's biggest secret."

"Hey, we all got secrets here. To trust each other, we got to have mutual assured rat outs. Like a Mexican standoff of secrets. You keep my secret, I'll keep yours."

Clay announced to Eddy in his deepest voice, "FYI, we have an officer of the law here. Sheriff Jim Osborne."

This took Eddy aback for a second. But Jim jumped in, "I'm not with Immigration. I'm just here to keep the peace. And tonight I'm just here to have a good time. I'm off duty."

"Way off duty I'd say," said Clay with a wink, noting that Jim had a bottle of beer in each hand.

"Beggin' your pardon, sir, but you already have knowledge of aliens," said Eddy in an almost accusatory voice, as if pointing out some deep corruption or moral flaw.

"Why don't we change the subject?" I pleaded.

Doc had to put in the last word. "Well, then, looks like we have a room full of outlaws, illegals, musicians of questionable repute, an even stranger being waiting in the wings somewhere, plus a couple of ordinary-looking people to fill out the audience. And one lawman to keep the peace. Sounds like we're well on our way to having a rock concert! "

Eddy turned to his drummer. "Carlos, let me help you set up your gear.

My house has one large central room that is living room, dining room, library, and music studio all in one, with a deck along the front overlooking the ocean. I've always been light on furniture, and it's all on casters, so it was easy to put the big pieces out on the deck, through the sliding-glass doors. We pulled in the flop-back easy chairs for the audience, and left one end of the room open for the musicians. On my walls near the ceiling are four speakers, plenty big to rattle windows and permanently damage your hearing.

I had trained Clay to be my substitute sound engineer for nearby gigs where I didn't have the budget to hire anybody. We set up the mikes, and he manned the mixer all evening, adjusting the sliders to capture this odd mix of voices and music.

Eddy had two guitars: an acoustic with electrical hookup, and a classic Stratocaster worthy of Jimi Hendrix. Using a dolly, he lugged in an amp that could fill the Coliseum with music. I silently thanked the previous owner of this house (may he rest in peace) for the extra fifty-amp circuits he had installed for the grow lights he needed for his "crop."

I had to hook up Gibb to a mike so that Eddy wouldn't drown me out.

Lucky for me that my neighbors on each side, Clay and the Osbornes, were my good friends and were here, because some of this sound would flood out over the countryside. Who knows, the whales swimming down the coast might sing along.

The evening turned out to be a bit of a potluck, even though I hadn't planned it that way. Catering is not my forte. Everybody brought a little something to nosh on and something to sip—or gulp. Eddy brought his standard bottle of Cabo Wabo tequila—plus a bottle of rum. Doc brought a six-pack of his favorite IPA, Heinously Hoppy. Jim brought his Bud Lite. Meg had her bottle of white zin, plus some fizzy water. Clay and me shared our favorite Argentinean Torrontes and Malbec.

Carlos? He sucked on a doobie all night. Generated a nice haze of second-hand smoke. Meg coughed a couple of times and tried to fan it away. But later, the way her mood lightened up, she may have gotten a wee bit high.

Finally, I brought forth the guest of honor from my bedroom where she'd been watching a National Geographic animal show on TV.

When I led her into the big room where everybody was sitting around, she was more than excited. Tooting and chiming and jiggling in anticipation. But looking around seeing everybody, she hung back a moment. Stage fright? Hard for me to tell if her quivering was excitement or nervousness.

Everybody stared at her, and she stared back. Complete silence.

"This is my friend Breadbox. That's my nickname for her. On her world, she is known as Bvar-nala-gna, which I can almost pronounce. She has learned some English words, but she uses a translating device, which she carries with her. She's not here to give a speech, but to sing.

"Breadbox, this man is Eddy. Eddy Backwater. And his friend Carlos.

"Pleased to meet you," she squeaked in English. Then she added in her language, using Wanda as translator, "I recall Eddy Backwater from earlier music event."

When Wanda had first started translating for Breadbox, the voice was metallic and unisex and monotone, and mixed up consonants. But her voice had developed into a rich alto feminine voice that spoke pretty good English and was full of expression.

Wanda beepled something to Breadbox, who then said to us via Wanda, "My device tells me that eddy and backwater mean the same thing. You have a double name. Is this related to your music?"

"Oh, little person, you have gone straight to my greatest secret. Eddy Backwater is my stage name, like a nickname."

"Then you must also have a secret name that only your family knows."

"Yes, 'fraid so, and even they have probably forgot it by now."

"I do not ask that you tell it."

"And I won't blow your cover, Eddy," I added sardonically.

"On my world, being one who sings to others is a very high honor. Singing is a . . . sacred . . . activity, and also for pure joy and pleasure." She said something to me in Fedi, and also beepled to Wanda. Wanda explained. "Sacred is a word of your world that is close to our word for 'deepest meaning.' Singing and dancing are for expressing the deepest meaning with joy and pleasure." Wanda used a different voice for her "personal" statements—like this brief explanation—from when she was translating Breadbox.

"Amen to that," chimed in Eddy.

"And those fortunate enough to bring deep meaning with joy and pleasure are honored by others," added Breadbox. "I was chosen for that role by my people. That's what I gave up to come to this world."

The melody for "Cotton Candy Lovin'" coursed through my mind. Sacred? Deepest meaning? More like no meaning. I felt embarrassment for myself. I must have gone beet red. For years, I had been just a cotton candy singer, eschewing deep meaning. Thus constricting my pleasure and enjoyment. And now my honored guest was admitting to everybody that she had done the same thing.

I said as much to my guests. Meg, of all people, sprang to my defense. "I don't think that's true, Selena. 'Cotton Candy Lovin' has deep meaning, especially to a lot of women. I don't think I ever told you this. Maybe not even you, Jim. Years ago, when I first heard 'Cotton Candy Lovin', I was about to make just that kind of choice for myself, because I was feeling so lonely. But, Selena, your song jolted me out of that. I decided right then and there that I was going to wait for my tall, gangly policeman-in-training." She leaned over and gave Jim a peck on the cheek. He was embarrassed, but he beamed with pride, and squeezed her hand.

"Enlightenment is where you find it," put in Clay.

I was flabbergasted. I had never had feedback like this about my signature song, a song that I had despised, but which had bought me my house on the coast. I had always viewed it as my pact with the devil, but here now was an angelic twist.

Eddy agreed with Meg. "You know, I sing these dumb yahoo country lyrics, and make a joke out of it. But I know from the tears in the eyes of those ladies—and men—singing along with me that I'm tapping into something real for them. Do you think all these people would have paid for your music if it was truly just cotton candy?"

My mind whirled with thoughts and feelings that I couldn't express. My singing, which had become rote to me, was still new to my audiences. Or, even if they'd heard it a hundred times before, it still resonated with them. They weren't coming to hear me because I was same ole same ole. How interesting. I needed to cogitate on that.

"Breadbox," asked Meg, "are you going to sing us a song from your world?

"Gladly will I sing such a song," she said through Wanda. "But first," she turned her eye stalks toward Eddy, and then me, "I want to sing some of your music with you."

Her tentacles danced in a complex waving pattern. "I rejected my Choice to sing on my world. What is the stroke of cosmic chance that brought me across the starstream to this one world? Here I am now. I have the great fortune and privilege to connect with singers of deep meaning and pleasure on a completely new world. None is more honored than I. I shall now fulfill my Choice. I choose to be here and sing with you."

"And so also do I choose," I said, laying my hand on the outstretched tentacle of Breadbox.

"That goes for me too!" shouted Eddy, pumping his fist. "So enough of this chatter. Let the music begin!"

He picked up his Stratocaster, and I readied my ears for a blast of sound, but instead, he laid down this very soft and gentle line, like a ballad. Carlos quickly followed with the brushes. After a few bars, Breadbox came in with a counterpoint, sounding like a soft oboe. It was enchanting.

"Clay, did you remember to start the audio recording?" I asked.

"My dear, I have been recording this entire evening. Video also. There's not a second to be missed of this event."

Then Eddy segued into one of his classics.

> *I ain't got no girl*
> *I ain't got no love*
> *I ain't got no nothin'*
> *Heavens above*
>
> *I don't want nothin'*
> *'Cept a little love*
> *But I can't find none*
> *Heavens above*

> *Let me pause now, and sit while I wail*
> *And let my geetar tell my sad tale.*

Then his "big gun," as he called his Stratocaster, opened up, and did just wail. Eddy can make a guitar cry—and his sobbed, and whimpered, and moaned.

Breadbox jumped right in with her organ voice and echoed every guitar wail.

I was so glad I had readied my flute, and even practiced on it a little bit. I picked up their line and built on it. If Breadbox's organ chords were the alto part, I was the high soprano. We had a three-part round. Eddy would lay it down, Breadbox would repeat and elaborate, then I would come in on top with a shrill counterpoint.

Then Eddy switched to the bass rhythm. Breadbox and I played off each other, and I started voicing over the flute, kind of growling, like an old Jethro Tull track.

Carlos was a magician on percussion. He played like he was an extension of his drums. He put down a jazz rhythm behind us, not a driving rock beat. Smooth and liquid, like butter and cream. Brought tears to my eyes just listening to him. Where was he from? How come I'd never heard of him before?

I growled that flute as low as it would go, then I laid it down and stepped up to the mike to sing. I just made it up as I went along. Lucky we were recording it, because I didn't know what the hell I was singing.

> *When impossibility calls your name, my friend,*
> *You better listen up*
> *When impossibility calls your name*

Jam session

You better step right up
This night is impossible, can not happen
yet here we are all the same.
We better know what's up.

We are here, tossed together
from hither and wherever
We're all in this together,
singing out our hearts.
Singing out our hearts, oh yeah,
till the rising of the sun.
We sing with love and zest
with those we know the best
till the rising of the sun.

And also, I say,
with those we know hardly at all.
Our song brings out new selves within
that we never knew had a real hope of life.
Ah, joy and pleasure at meeting new friends
and those we've known most all of our life.
Yes, including our own narrow lives.
"Now let's bring it back home . . .
Including my own narrow life, did I say?
Who am I? Always thought that I knew.
But that notion is gone, it's twisted askew.
I'm so much more than what I have known
As you've shown me tonight 'neath the glorious moon
I can deny it no more, my new self, my new day.

They actually applauded for me!

Then Breadbox and I did Together Stars People, which was my adaptation of her melody. The one I had done at Point Arena, where her sing-along had caught Eddy's notice. She did the melody with her soft organ voice, and I sang.

Standing ovations are wonderful even with just a handful of people.

"Breadbox, would you now like to sing us a song from your world?" I asked her gently.

"The music we sing among our people is very different from yours. Not as joyous. Not so full of energy and feeling."

"Together Stars People, which we just did, was a melody of yours." I didn't want to push her too hard.

"Oh no, that is yours. I would do a very old song from my world, that we sing to remind ourselves who we really are, and what our place is."

Everybody nodded encouragement.

104

"Best if we go outside under the stars and contemplate the limitless black sky."

Everybody shuffled out onto the deck. Breadbox crawled out, dodging people's legs, and looked out through the bars of the deck railing at the black ocean. She held Wanda so that people could hear the translation of the song. Breadbox intoned slowly in her language, and then in English, sounding like a Gregorian chant, "We are mournful. We are awestruck. We are accepting." Then she went into this slow song-poem.

Up to now, everything Breadbox had done was "instrumental," using her various voices. On this one, she sang the words in the language I had come to recognize as Fedi. Soft and lyrical, not in the musical scale we are accustomed to. She could sing multiple notes at once, using more than one scale. It definitely sounded alien, eerie and beautiful.

She also moved in this graceful dance, with all her tentacles (except the one that cradled Wanda) waving in synchrony, like a multi-armed goddess doing a hula. The colors of her skin rippled along with the movements of her tentacles.

I was astounded at Wanda's ability to translate into English as Breadbox sang, and to retain much of the poetic rhythm of the song. Breadbox held Wanda near her head, so the sounds seemed to come from the same place.

The universe is cold and uncaring
life is a nothingful scum.

We life, we call ourselves smart ones;
we use our brave tools
to guide our smart pebbles
from sun to sun to sun.

We build our temples and towers,
our passions and stories,
our shames, our wars,
our conquests and glories
while starwheels spin uncaring above.

We life, we always crave meaning
where no meaning can ever be found.
So let us create some meaning
just to keep ourselves happy and found
and to build our short lives around.

Thus we sing and continue the story
the most valuable gem that we hold.
Tell our fleeting hope and our glory.

If song dies, so too dies our meaning
so sing it till heavens grow cold.

Then she sang a reprise with a much more upbeat rhythm.

So, let us light a spark
and share it now together
I ask you: come share my light
my warmth and song
Let's tell tall tales, sip a warm mug,
and laugh the whole night long
In the morn sun, a hug,
a cup of brew
to rekindle our warmth
in the cool of early dew.

Breadbox was silent a moment, then intoned solemnly with her tentacles crossed in a gesture of supplication, "Accept my ode to our friendship and our joy of singing together."

Complete silence. This had been totally out of this world, both message and melody. A sacred hymn from a godless world. Challenging in its message. I could see Doc frowning, Clay nodding—both thoughtfully.

Jim had his arm around Meg, who was huddling against him and crying. Eddy was scribbling in a small spiral notebook he'd pulled out of his jacket pocket. Composing a song based on what she'd sung? Carlos had not come out onto the deck, but still sat behind his drums, practicing a soft counterpoint to her music.

And me? A song was pushing at the back of my mind, asking to be born. My response to her message. I took up the mike again.

'Cross all the worlds, across all space
The song of love has but one face.
I see your face, I see your love
I hear your voice, I hear your song
The sacred song of everywhere
With thee this night I share.

May those on all the worlds we know
And others that lie beyond
Pick up our hymn, our sacred song
And know that they are part of it
And know that we are one.
Amen.

It was hard to go back to rock or country after that, so the jam session wound down. Eddy and Carlos spent a few minutes trying out a few chords and riffs together, loosely based on Breadbox's melody.

Nobody had much to say. Clay and Doc pulled the big sofa back into the living room from the deck, so people had space to flop down. Breadbox climbed onto my big ottoman next to the sofa, right in the middle of the room.

As jam sessions go, this one had been totally unique.

24. The After Party

Even after the jam session wound down, people stayed around working on Eddy's bottle of Cabo Wabo.

Eddy jumped right into his main idea. "Why don't you take Breadbox out on the road? That would be the biggest music sensation ever. I want to go with you. This will be the tour of a lifetime. You don't have to pay me—in fact, I'd pay you to go."

Jim added, "You might as well. You know you can't keep this a secret forever."

"Yeah, but I have no interest in creating this freak-show atmosphere," I said.

"If Selena did that," countered Doc, "then the whole thing is blown open. Everybody, including the government, will know about the spaceship. Do you think for a minute they will let you keep it?"

Clay looked at me. "Okay, so what are your plans for it? You want to open a space museum on your back hill?"

"I've always had in mind fixing it up so that Breadbox could return home, and take the remains of her crewmembers."

Eddy giggled at this. "Have you contacted any flying saucer body shop and repair services?" He and Carlos were trading hits on a joint.

"What do you care about the spaceship?" asked Meg. "It's just a ruined hulk. Better to let them have it. Maybe they can learn something useful."

Clay nodded agreement. "I was thinking the same thing. If these so-called alien 'kids' got here, then eventually the 'grown ups' will follow. And who knows what their intentions will be? Seems smart to see what we can learn from their technology, in case we have to defend ourselves."

"It's a matter of timing," I replied.

Clay intoned, "The clock is ticking.

I shook my head and looked at my hands. "I cannot subject Breadbox to the stress of a music tour. She's not strong enough. She needs to stay close to her life support. Look, if they take the ship, they have to take Breadbox also. She depends on that tube that feeds her."

At this point, Breadbox blasted out an organ chord. She had been completely left out of this conversation, even though we were talking about her. What I had somehow forgotten, until she piped up, was that Wanda had been translating for her everything we said.

She sang a little ditty in her strongest organ-pipe voice, and Wanda translated to English.

"Greatest desire to go sing. Love singing. Love singing with people, with musical devices. Tonight was the best time. Please take me singing!" She then did this instrumental (meaning non-verbal) riff, starting out in my style, then merging over to Eddy's. One piece of music that bridged both of us. It was phenomenal!

We all just sat there, mouth-agape speechless.

Eddy said, "Your alien has spoken, loud and clear."

Clay added, "If you just wait and do nothing, eventually you'll lose control of the situation. Better for you to go public while things are in your control. World tour with the first alien musician. It will be harder for them to take her away from you once you've gone public and have generated lots of publicity."

Eddy gave a thumbs up. "Yeah, especially with the music."

Doc countered, "I don't believe that for a second. They'll swoop in and take her away on some pretext. And the spaceship."

"Wait a minute." I shook my head. "Breadbox is not asking to go on a world tour. She wants to sing with people. Like tonight. We don't have to expose her to insane crowds who would want to swarm all over her. Or attack her."

"You don't have to travel nowhere!" Eddy expostulated, jumping up in front of me. "Bring the world to you. You've got a studio right here."

I must admit, this crazy idea did have a certain appeal to me. This would be a way for me to put forth some of my special music that I had been holding back. Her music and my pieces inspired by hers. I wouldn't have to be concerned about the commercial potential of my music, the way I'd always been. I'd be riding the wave of popularity of Breadbox's music.

But I could not see how it would be possible to do this just for cheap thrills, without risking her health and well-being and safety—even though I knew she wanted to do it.

I was mulling this over long after everybody went home. Breadbox seemed exhausted by the evening. She pulled in her tentacles and went to sleep as I was wheelbarrowing her back to the comfort of her crashed spaceship, as the midnight stars looked on. I helped her up onto her gurney as she clasped Wanda, and I connected her life-support tube for her. I spread her favorite horse blanket over her and Wanda, said goodnight, and gave her an air kiss. She raised one eyestalk part way and squeaked in English, "Thank you, my best friend."

25. The Choice

"**B**ullshit! Everything I have told you is bull!" I ranted.

"Bull? What is bull?" asked Breadbox. Wanda beepled to her, then gave a tentative back translation in English. "The feces of a large male grazing quadruped, sometimes dangerous."

"I meant wrong. Incorrect. Untruthful. I lied to you. And to myself about why I am a musician."

I had awakened at 3:00am, my normal angst time, angry at myself. The truth became clear to me, and I now repeated it to Breadbox. We were back at her crash-site abode beneath the big oak, even before breakfast, the morning after the jam session. "One does not become a musician, but rather, realizes she is one. It's all I ever wanted to do. I just am a musician. I would be one even if I didn't make a living at it."

I could have kept music as a hobby and done something else instead, but the right doors opened at the right time, and I ended up doing music. I heard Bonnie Raitt and Melissa Etheridge and I thought, that's what I want to do.

I paused and looked at my fingers playing an imaginary guitar. "It's an amazing gift that I get to travel around and sing to total strangers."

I laughed out loud. Laughed and hooted and cried. Tears of joy and sadness. Joy of realization and release, sadness for years lost. "Last night you and I both chose again to be singers, did we not? After all the moaning and denying, the truth came out in our jam with our friends."

"Yes, I chose," she asserted, with twirling tentacles and flashing purple skin spots. She did a little skipping dance, with six or eight of her feet, like those Irish troupes do, but she was the whole troupe. "I chose to sing with you and your friends. I loved singing along with your friend Backwater. I love his double name. Backwater or eddy is the still part of the stream, quiet, out away from the rushing current."

"That seems just the opposite of what he is."

"Perhaps his name expresses his quiet inner self."

I smirked to myself, trying to imagine Eddy with a quiet inner self. But then, what about me? I'd been hiding my inner self pretty well. Mostly from myself. Not wanting to admit who I was, and where my passion really lay. Because if I did admit it, then I'd have to do something about it. I'd have to sing my passion without holding back. Despite my fear of rejection.

But Breadbox had stirred my passion kettle, and stimulated me to sing it all out. And people had loved it! I was amazed; it was hard for me to grant this. They liked my singing from the heart. Loved it! Stood up and applauded. Asked to record and produce it. Ah, Joel.

I had long been a successful singer. Hit songs. Concerts. Albums. Lots of money. Beautiful home overlooking the ocean. But I'd never felt successful to myself. I'd ridden the safety of my early hits, slowly downhill it seemed. I was never satisfied with my recent hits. They seemed clever but derivative, contrived to be popular. And they were popular, but . . .

Further, I'd been a total failure at finding and keeping a true love in my life. Heck, cotton candy lovin' would be a step up for me! Even Joel. He didn't even want a fling with me.

"What is the role of the singer in your world?" Breadbox had asked me once.

"It is to entertain," I had told her. And yet, I asked myself now, why are these songs entertaining? I see that songs carry profound meaning and lessons for people. Things they need to learn in their own lives. Or that resonate with problems they experience. They need this external force—music—playing this back to them. What was brought home to me, particularly by Meg last night, was that things a singer like me might consider trivial and humdrum, the listener might find moving and profound. Maybe the lyrics, maybe the melody. Or maybe the setting, like that magical evening recently up at Point Arena.

Perhaps I feared being too successful. I didn't feel qualified to be messing with people's lives and happiness. That's quite a responsibility. It's like I needed to be an expert surgeon, but I hardly knew how to wield the scalpel. So I held back.

Sounds contradictory, doesn't it? I feared nobody would care, and I feared that I'd have too great an impact. Well, that was me.

I couldn't yet verbalize all this to Breadbox, so instead I asked her a question.

"Why did you refuse your Choice to be a singer? You are such a natural-born singer." I was amazed I'd never asked her this before.

She didn't answer immediately. She ambled over to the gravesites of her two crew partners, and briefly touched her head to each of the markers I had placed. She looked at the sky and held her tentacles in a particular pose, as if praying. Then she turned back to me.

"As you observe, I am a singer. I have been singing all the time since I have been here on your world. I rebelled against being forced to choose— to choose singing in a particular way."

Then she changed the subject. "Agate, my friend, I understand you recorded our music last night. May I hear some of it again?"

"Of course. Let's go down to my house. Then I can get something to eat, also."

"I am so sorry to deprive you of your sustenance."

"No, no. No apology needed. I'm in no danger of starving."

She climbed into the wheelbarrow and I grunted with the effort of pushing her up to the lip of the gully, then restraining it from getting away from me as we went down the steep, bumpy hill to my house. Transporting her this way was a great full-body workout for me. I knew, because I kept checking my abs and biceps in the mirror. But next time, perhaps I'd let her walk on her own.

As we clunked down the hill, she went on. "We both sing from our hearts and passion. We sing our own music. We sing with our friends. On my world, the singer's role is to reinforce the messages that the Elders wish to convey. That wasn't enough for me. I wanted more than that."

When we got to my house, I gobbled some of the leftover snacks from last night while I cued up the recordings Clay had done, including the video. I left greasy fingerprints all over my equipment.

Breadbox was spellbound. "I have never before viewed myself while singing. It is so strange hearing these sounds of mine."

"You sound very good."

"We sound well together. And Backwater also."

"I admire Wanda for being able to translate not just language, but also song, and to be your voice."

"Yes, this device has so many functions," she agreed, caressing it. "Agate, my dearest friend, if anything should ever happen to me, might I entrust you with my device, that you call Wanda the Wand? I have communicated this to it."

"What do you think is going to happen to you? I am going to help you thrive until we can find a way to repair your vessel so you can return home."

She didn't answer for some time. "Agate, my best friend, I see no evidence that my vessel can be repaired on this world. Many pieces are missing. Even if it could be, I would not be able to pilot it home without my crew, who, alas, are dead. And I cannot return because of my shame and disgrace due to the circumstances of my departure."

I insisted that she was in good health, and that it was improving. But I had noticed that the aqua patches of her skin were fading a bit, and appearing grayer. More gray skin, less bright color. "You are looking a little gray around the throat. I'm worried that you are losing color."

"Don't worry about me. I am doing very well. This is the best it has ever been in my life."

Hmm. I'd have to keep close watch on her.

I asked about the piece she had sung. "What kind of a melody was it?"

"A common hymn that everybody knows. But it is never sung the same way twice. There is no standard lyric or melody. Every time it is

112

sung, it will be slightly different."

"Do your people record their music, as we do here?"

"Generally not, because the purpose of the music is to create a live experience."

"Do groups of people sing together?"

"Oh yes, all the time. One of the roles of the Chosen Singer is to lead this singing, and coordinate, to teach others the songs. We put on large events that include many groups singing, one after another."

"What kind of songs? What are the themes?"

"The purpose of the songs is to carry the spirit of our people. We sing songs of our place in the universe, like the one I sang last night. To remind people of our glorious past, and the limitations of the present. We sing the songs of our clan. Each clan has its own melodies.

"We all mass in different locations, on small hills, or flat plazas, or raised platforms, or atop structures. We have a chorus of choruses.

"You must understand that for us, singing includes movement, what you call dance. These are not separate for our people. I have not exhibited my movement side very much, because I have been physically unable. Or constrained to my bed you prepared for me due to my physical weakness. And the music hasn't been the proper kind."

"This sounds beautiful! I would love to see it. You could be our 'chosen singer' here and teach our people to sing and dance that way."

She heartily agreed by doing a wiggling jig.

"But I don't understand. If it is your role to conduct this wondrous singing, why did you refuse it?"

"It is wondrous to behold to an outside observer. But my role as the Chosen Singer would be to constrain the freedom of the singing, and make sure it stays in prescribed channels. The singer's role is to reinforce the messages that the Elders wish to convey," she repeated what she'd said earlier. "That wasn't enough for me. I wanted more than that."

Breadbox did her tentacle wave that signified ambivalence or uncertainty, or the need to say something difficult. Her skin spots fluctuated in color.

"There is one more thing that happened to me. I was sent to a distant world to study song. That's when I discovered I was being groomed for this special role. While there, I worked with a young male from that world. He and I became very close friends. He had a large beak and beautiful wispy feathers the color of the early morning sky. He sang and trilled wondrously. He created many songs expressing his affection for me, and I likewise for him. Our voices and modes of singing were so very different, yet we learned to combine them and sing in harmony. We danced intricate patterns as we sang. I waved and twirled my song tentacles, and he rippled his long back feathers. We were as different as you and me, but we sang as one. And our feeling was deep and mutual.

"We were discovered. My clan overseers were outraged that I allowed myself to have a relationship of love with an alien being. How could I fulfill my designated role if I nurtured my feelings for this strange being? This is what they said to me."

"I thought the peoples of different worlds in your Confederation treated one another as equals."

"Yes, this is so in many spheres of behavior. But many oki races, mine in particular, deem it a taboo to form strong personal relationships with other races. There have been very bad experiences with different oki races trying to crossbreed. Not that that was ever our intention. But I may never have been able to find a mate of my own people if I had consorted with such a being.

"I was forced to renounce him. His clan likewise punished him, though I do not know the details, because I have never since had any contact with him.

"My spirit was crushed. I could do nothing but throw myself into intensive study of song, but only with the part of me that analyzes and learns. Not with my laughing and loving and singing spirit. Thereafter I sought to rekindle the spirit of singing, but with little success."

"Wow, this is unbelievable. How come you never told me this before?"

"I am so sorry, my best friend, that I have been unable to share this sad tale with you. It has been beyond my strength."

"It is uncanny how alike you and I are. What force in the Universe brought us together?"

"It is only with you that I have been once again able to release my spirit. I have fulfilled my choice. I am happy. I am complete. I am now at peace."

For a moment, I puzzled about what conscious force had reached out across the cosmic void to connect two lovelorn females. And singers at that. No, I doubted that our plights were all that unique. How many gazillions of beings seek love and passion? Ah, I thought, we need to launch the "interstellar love connection." Could be my next venture.

"You have become close friends with beings of two completely different races. Maybe others you haven't mentioned. You are what your Confederation claims to be about—the brotherhood of all intelligent beings. Yet you have been punished and constrained for this. Seems like cosmic hypocrisy to me."

"Let us not discuss this further," she said. "I wanted you to understand. But now I would like to discuss how we can sing more together, as we did with your friends."

"It is their idea—especially Eddy's—that we sing in front of many more people. A concert." I shook my head no, then nodded yes, in total uncertainty and ambivalence. I must have looked like a bobblehead doll.

"I would like that."

"But I am not willing to take you to distant places. You're not strong enough." I was frowning. "And people are not accustomed to your appearance."

"I understand that. I cannot stray far from my life support. But could we bring people to us? Could we use your television in reverse, so that others quite distant could view us while we perform? I would not mind that. It would allow me to fulfill my destiny, even though here on your world. My destiny now is to sing with you, and with Backwater, and with others."

She was so excited, she was doing a little jig. The color returned to her skin patches. "Let's plan our next music event."

OMG, had I just been roped into a musical partnership with Crazy Eddy? And Sad Carlos the alien? I know that's exactly what Eddy wanted. Looks like he had wangled his way in by cozying up to my friend. It would be very hard for me to say no to Breadbox.

In the bathroom, I glanced at the mirror. I hardly recognized myself. I looked so happy, joyous, younger even. Like just after wonderful sex. My skin tone was improved. No gray patches at all. The happiness of knowing who I am, and liking it.

26. My Best Friend Is Gone

She dropped in on my house one day
And I truly thought she was here to stay
Funny looking, cannot talk
But hoots and chimes and honks and squawks
How can such beings with nothing in common
Develop such a bond
  From Inner-Galactic Journey album

No warning—she just died. We were at my house—far from her life support—listening to my albums with the volume turned up to window rattler. She made a little swirl gesture with two intertwined tentacles, then went still. I sat and stared, in shock. Then I smacked her metallic midriff, like you would a balky appliance, to jolt her back to life. I wanted to do CPR.

But she was gone. One moment she was my bosom buddy with whom I shared my secret songs and deepest secrets. The next she was a lifeless squid sticking out of a large tin can. I cried, I shrieked, I keened with grief. I sat in shocked stupor way into the evening.

For months, I had devoted my life to nursing this frail being back to health so that she could summon some of her kind to come retrieve her from this distant, alien world. I had scoffed at her doubts and denials. I had ignored that she knew she was dying. She had hinted that she wanted me to convey her story back to her clan. That's why she had been trying to teach me to use the wand.

She'd been doing so well. We'd taken all these field trips, and she seemed more and more energized. As I looked back, I spotted warning signs I had overlooked. The times she had trembled and whimpered. I had noticed her bright skin patches getting duller, and the pallor around the base of her head.

But she was so eager to experience things. I wanted to give her what she wanted, let her do what she wanted to do. I had been her friend and social director, not a professional looking out for the well-being of this unique entity.

We'd been having so much fun. She was like a cross between my old dog Buddy and the kid I'd never had. And she was a singer! She loved my music! I'd had fantasies of introducing her to the world, forming a musical duet and going on tour.

How selfish of me. This had been all about me, not her well-being. I was floored by a wave of guilt and grief.

Earth had been slowly killing Breadbox, I believe. Too much gravity, perhaps; too much oxygen. She had been slowly starving to death. Malnutrition? I had asked her if she couldn't calibrate the remaining life-support system to produce what she needed. She was silent, then granted that yes, it probably could. It's as if she didn't care whether it did or not. That's spiritual malaise in my book, or even clinical depression.

The turning point had come, I realized looking back, when she discovered that the engine of her vessel was missing and had perhaps been one of the pieces fallen into the Pacific Ocean. "The engine that moves us," she had said. Breadbox had wanted to show it to me, so we crawled back through the tunnel, past the ruined crew quarters, through all the debris. Breadbox pointed further back. "It's gone!" she trilled with Wanda's translation, but I could hear the frustration directly.

Till that time, she could hope her vessel could be repaired over time and could take her home. After she had discovered it was missing, her mood had changed. That's when she had become willing to leave the security of her life-support system and come visit my house. As she had told me, she'd chosen to be with me and be a singer here on Earth. I'm sure she was genuinely happy, even though she had given up hope of returning home, and knew that this was her final resting place.

Around midnight, under the light of Jupiter high in the sky, I buried her in the artichoke patch—the only place near my house I had enough decent soil to bury anybody. But I was crying so hard I could scarcely see to dig. My heart was pounding with the effort and the grief. She would be right next to Buddy, my other non-human family member. I buried her in the last of the body bags Doc had brought. I wrapped her wand in a separate garbage bag and laid it on top of her. Then I filled in the hole.

I pulled over my old yard chair that I sit on to watch the garden grow, and I talked to her. I cajoled. I berated. I told her I loved her.

After a pause, I admitted to her that I was not going to try to contact her people. Her wand would stay buried.

I sang. All the melodies I had shared with her and with no one else. I got Gibb from my bedroom and we sang together.

But I confess: In the midst of my grief, I did have the presence of mind to turn on my digital recorder and mikes. I've done some of my best recording sessions in the wee hours, crying over lost love.

* * *

In the morning, I told the others. Actually, I summoned them, and they all came right over. We stood around my back garden where I had buried Breadbox, and held an impromptu wake for her. I passed around a six-pack of beer. We took turns remembering things about her. Her delight in all the things we showed her and taught her. Her utter joy during the jam session, singing with Eddy and me.

They took their cue from my mood and were quite subdued, but their reactions were mixed.

"I am so sorry for you, Selena," said Clay. "I know how much it, I mean she, meant to you. You've put so much into this." Pause. "I'm amazed she lasted this long."

Sheriff Jim pursed his lips. "I must confess, I am relieved this is over. I've been feeling the strain of keeping this hidden." This hurt my feelings a bit, but I could sure see that this was true for him.

Meg gave me a hug then said, "It's terrible! We should have turned her over to the authorities. They may have been able to save her."

Doc retorted with vehemence, "No! We did our best. Those government yahoos would have done no more."

I said something sappy like "I love all of you, and I thank you so much for your support through all of this. I apologize for creating such a huge burden on you. So many demands."

Then we did a big group hug, even the big ole hard-nosed men.

"It's been one hell of a trip," Doc said. "Are you going to write this up?"

"Yes indeed," I nodded emphatically, "but in music."

After a pause, Clay said, "What are we going to do with the ship?"

Silence. Oh yeah, we still had a hundred-ton hunk of alien technology hidden up the hill under the big oak tree. We all turned to look up the hill toward it, even though we couldn't see it from the garden.

"First thing we have to do is clean things up," I pointed out in my motherly tone of voice. "Doc, you've got half a clinic's worth of stuff up there under my oak tree. I'll help you retrieve it."

We all went up to the vessel and removed everything we had brought up there. lugging it up to our various vans and trucks. I was embarrassed that the biggest cleanup task was hauling out my accumulated midden—aka trash—of paper plates and beer bottles and related detritus.

I was sobbing and bawling the whole time. We kept taking breaks for them to comfort me and give me hugs. I noticed that even the tough old guys were secretly wiping tears from their faces.

"One other thing you should clean up," reminded Doc when we all assembled back at my house. "You've got all these photos and videos and audio recordings of your visitor. You should gather all of those in one place. One secure place. You don't want those strewn all over the place on hackable phones and cameras and computers."

As we finished up and mopped the sweat from our brows, Sheriff Jim said quietly, "Maybe now's the time to turn it over the to authorities."

"Not so fast!" countered Doc. "Doesn't this belong to Selena? After all, it's on her property. Just like a meteorite. If it falls from the sky onto your property, it's yours."

Clay added, "It will be worth a fortune!"

I weighed in. "You know, guys, what I always wanted to do was find a way to get it repaired so that she could return home."

"Fix it up?" scoffed Clay, my supposed ally. "That's crazy! Pieces strewn all over the place, and it looks like a major part is missing. Blown to smithereens, or burned up in the atmosphere, or fell into the ocean."

"Now that she's dead, fixing it up makes no sense," I admitted. "But I have no other plan."

Doc scowled; the others nodded in agreement.

"Well, I don't have to decide just yet," I said as they ambled toward my driveway for their cars. "I'm going to sleep on it."

After they left, I did what I'd been planning to do yesterday—plant new artichokes. Now planted to honor a new member of the garden. I also followed Doc's advice and backed up all my recordings of Breadbox into a secured site in the cloud.

Maybe Meg had been right. I was having chooser's remorse. I had made what I thought was the right choice, and it had worked out poorly. My face flushed with guilt.

Standing by her grave, I made a vow to her. "Breadbox, my best friend, my Choice is that from now on I will put all my music out there, and hold nothing back."

What about her ship? "I'm going to sleep on it," I had said. It turned out, I slept on it a bit too long.

27. All Hell Breaks Loose

This party's over folks
The food and booze are gone
Just gather up your stuff now
And head on out to home
From "Back to Real Life" on Inner-Galactic Journey album

Two weeks later I was awakened at dawn by an invading horde. The vessel had been spotted by the pilot of a small plane, and reported. The amazing thing is that it went undiscovered as long as it did.

My life had basically ground to a halt after Breadbox's death. I knew I needed to make some decisions about the spaceship and take some action, but I was essentially catatonic. Grieving and crying. Clay, and even Doc, did their best to comfort me, but I wasn't very good company. I was inconsolable. What I didn't realize, in my grief, was that they were grieving also.

My stages of grief were rudely interrupted.

One day all was calm and tranquil. The next my hillside was aswarm with Humvees and helicopters and white vans with odd equipment. Exactly like that old "ET Phone Home" movie, with men in white hazmat suits stringing yellow crime-scene tape everywhere.

Nobody had knocked on my door to ask permission. They just bulled their way up along the north edge of my property with big trucks. I hoped they all got a good dose of poison oak! When someone finally did knock on my front door, which I never use, people in masks informed me I was to remain in place.

As they knocked, my landline rang at the same time. Hazmat suits at the door, FBI (they said) on the phone.

I was quarantined in my own house at first. "House arrest." My crime? "Harboring an illegal alien?" I wanted to ask them, in case any of them had a sense of humor. They didn't. I was never officially arrested. It was for "observation," in case I showed symptoms of some ghastly intergalactic disease. "Sequestered," they said. "Kidnapped" seemed more apt.

At first, my captors with hazmat suits avoided me as much as possible. They operated from a large, white, windowless bus parked in my driveway. They took air samples, breath samples, blood samples, stool samples, and DNA samples, all gingerly as if they were the bomb squad and I was the ticking bomb. My objections didn't faze them. "It will be a lot better if you sign this waiver, so we don't have to take you in."

They took my cell phone, iPad, and laptop. "We want to see who you've been contacting."

"You don't need my phone for that."

"Well, we'll give it right back to you." But they kept forgetting to bring it back. Obviously their intent was to prevent me from contacting others.

I quickly discovered they'd also disconnected my landline. I could look out the windows, and also watch it all on TV. Police tape everywhere. Later I was spirited away to some unnamed windowless room, just like in spy movies. More on that in a bit.

Conspiracy theorists constantly accuse the government of hushing up their knowledge of the aliens and their plans. Ha! Fat chance! It was splashed all over Fox and CNN and BBC and Al Jazeera and every other channel. A million tweets at least.

As I sat captive in my own home, I got to watch the news ripple out across the nation and the world. It was drama and comedy, with a huge dose of farce.

My poor aliens that we had buried with dignity were roughly exhumed and hurried off in a van with flashing blue lights. They were easy to find because I had conveniently marked them with dated stones.

The reaction of the press to the alien incursion—and that of their readership, the population at large—was exactly what you would expect.

"This is the biggest story of our lifetimes—no—in all of history!"

"Alien invaders! What are their plans for Earth?"

"It's all a hoax, a fraud! This has all been carefully staged by our government to justify yet more inroads into our liberties."

"This is a message from God!" "No, from the Devil! Pray! Prepare to meet thy maker."

"Will they save us from ourselves with their masterful wisdom?"

Or, "Will we all end up in servitude to the alien masters?"

"Who is this diabolical woman on the West Coast? How did they choose her? What are they grooming her for?" Ha! Was I in league with them? Was I their chosen high priestess? Oh yes, bow down before me, you minions!

"These aliens in their flying saucers are causing all our big storms. They're dragging along the bad weather from their stars and messing up our atmosphere."

The stock market first tanked then rallied, as Wall Street swung from "It's the end of civilization as we know it" to "Wow! What a wonderful investment opportunity this could be!" The price of gold shot way up.

The press, plus various and sundry preachers, set up camp as close to my property as they could get. Farmer Jed made a killing renting out space in his woods above my property. I'm sure the paparazzi with their microphones and telephoto lenses on tripods were trampling all over the delicate habitat of endangered owls.

A previously unheralded Native American tribe said my property was actually on one of their ancient burial grounds, so they claimed the vessel for themselves. Rumor was they wanted to sell it and build a casino there.

The UN General Assembly debated the event and passed a resolution that whatever came from it had to be shared with the governments of every nation. They didn't say for the people or scientists of every nation—just for their governments, I noted with ironic glee. I could just see Doc nodding his head, smiling smugly, and saying, "See? I told you so."

Here's what became apparent over time. In most sci-fi stories about aliens encroaching on Earth, the role of government is to hush everything up and deny it ever happened. In this case, they did something that may have been even more clever, if not by design. No denials, just boring press releases. Kind of the "Nothing to see here folks, move along" approach. They buried their discoveries in long, dense texts, full of bafflegab.

In hindsight, I saw that the real story was more humdrum, even if in the long run more amazing. The leaked reports and boring press releases that emerged over the next few months, if you read them carefully, talked about new discoveries of materials from the vessel, the aliens' processes of space flight and how it would benefit our space program, new means of propulsion and sources of energy, the biology of the dead aliens and what that taught us about our own bodies. The first report comparing alien DNA with Earth's beings came out within two months.

I never saw any mention of advanced weaponry, even though that must have been at the top of the investigators' lists.

But right then, I was being held incommunicado in my own house. Even things happening up my back hill I only got to see on TV. I felt like a prisoner of war. I wondered if they planned to ship me off to Guantanamo in Cuba.

28. Quarantine. Incommunicado

When the man is a bully
And takes what is mine
And says to keep quiet
It was his all the time . . .
From "My Spaceship Calls Out to Me" on
Inner-Galactic Journey album

The dreaded midnight knock on my door came the night after the hazmat people took off their suits.

Late at night they came to take me away. Three men who looked like clones of Mr. Smith in The Matrix. They escorted me into a van with no windows. Drove at foolhardy speed down Highway 1. I couldn't see out to tell where we were going, but I did my best to track our movement by the twists and turns and traffic noise. All I could tell for sure was that we drove over back roads, then freeway, then over one of the bridges, probably the Richmond, which meant we were in the East Bay. Some more time on freeways, then local streets, then into a parking garage. Doors slid open. "Come this way, please." They hurried me into an elevator, zipped up several floors—five "dings" of the elevator—then out into a generic corridor. Into a room. Like a hotel room, except no windows. Desk, chairs, bed, kitchenette, bathroom. Big TV.

I guessed I was in Oakland. Where else in the near East Bay would a building with a number of floors be?

"Make yourself comfortable," growled Mr. Smith. "Someone will be here in the morning early." Then they left. I wasn't surprised to find out the door was locked from the outside.

I had brought nothing. There was a robe in the closet, a toothbrush—typical hotel amenities. A stupid one-cup powdered coffee maker with non-dairy creamer, yuck. Not even a chocolate mint on my pillow. I quickly discovered that the phone was disconnected.

I was angry and terrified, trembling and in shock. How could things like this happen? I wondered. I started to cry, then yelled at myself. "Cut this crap! You can't respond this way."

I turned on the TV to distract myself and to see if there were news flashes about my kidnapping. 2:35 am. No news, just insomniac programs.

123

That was me, that night. Too riled up and scared to sleep. I found an old rerun of Mystery Science Theater 3000, if you remember that program, where this geek and two robots make snide comments about a dumb movie. This one was about alien invaders who turned people into mindless zombies. Yikes! Too close to home! Just like my mindless zombie kidnappers. I settled for a Leave it to Beaver oldie.

I did doze off, because when I awoke the morning news was on, and I was treated to a helicopter view of my own property. The news guy talked about the unidentified vessel found on some unspecified farm, but never mentioned me. You could barely see the thing through the trees. From that vantage, it looked like some dark-gray shed. No wonder it had taken so long for it to be noticed.

The phone rang. So, it can take incoming calls. It was my wake-up call. A woman said, "It's 8 am. We want to talk with you at 9. We're sending up some breakfast. Do you have any dietary restrictions?" Only after I murmured no and she hung up did I think of all the smart-ass things I could have said. A faceless person wheeled in a cart with a breakfast burrito, orange juice, and a carafe of Starbucks with real half-and-half. I downed every crumb.

A youngish woman and a middle-aged, bureaucrat-looking man entered the room. He looked bored and embarrassed; she looked like a transplanted East German Stasi agent.

I sat in the room's only chair and left them standing.

Stasi: "Bertha Morris-ott?" Voice of a cop trying to intimidate a suspect. Impact dampened by the way she hashed my name.

"No, I'm Selena Morisot. I guess you have the wrong person."

Her: "Sez here your name is Bertha." Frowning at her smart phone. I had no idea what doc she was looking at.

"My birth name is Berthe. That's Bear-tuh, not Birth-a. And it's Mori-SO not Mori-SOTT." ("You ignorant yahoo," I didn't add.) "Who are you people?"

The man: "I'm Dr. Lew Spruce, and this is my partner Stacey Smith."

Ah, Mr. Smith's sister, I thought. I glowered at them. "Am I a prisoner of war?"

Her: "That depends. Are you an enemy combatant?"

"No, I'm a singer and composer. Maybe you're familiar with my music." That drew a blank.

Him: "Let's start over. We just need to ask you some questions."

"That's fine. As soon as you bring my lawyer up here."

Her: "Not just yet."

Him: "Before involving other people, we just want to talk with you a bit. Could you do that?" He spoke in a very accommodating way. "Perhaps you'd like to tell us in your own words what happened."

"Last night I was kidnapped from my house by three men and brought to this room against my will!"

Him: "I'm sorry about that. That was handled poorly. But right now we'd like to hear about the crashed vessel on your property."

"You had to kidnap me to ask me that?"

Her: "You were taken into custody because these actions have both public health and national security ramifications."

"National security?"

Her: "If, as seems likely, this is technology of an advanced extraterrestrial race, then your actions could have compromised public health and national security. You may have endangered us all. This could land you in jail."

Him: "No need for threats. Let me start by telling you what we already know." He confirmed they had found and dug up the two crewmembers. No mention of Breadbox, though, and I wasn't about to correct them. They had correlated the crash date with reports of the sonic boom. That led them to Sheriff Jim, and I was devastated to learn he had been suspended pending investigation. They told me they didn't buy his story in his report that he had inquired about the source of the sonic boom with all the coastal residents, but had discovered nothing.

"Don't you think it is your responsibility to protect others?" the woman asked me sternly, trying to make me feel guilty.

"I thought it was your responsibility to protect us," I countered. They were shifting back and forth, wishing they could sit, glancing at my bed. "Why aren't you protecting me? Yeah, it fell there. You needed me to tell you this? Where's your radar? You have all the instruments. It took you months to figure out it was there. And now you're telling me I might be

Interrogation

in danger? Yes, we found some things. We buried them, thought that was the best thing to do. I put them underground so nothing could get out of them. What was I supposed to do? I didn't want them to rot there on my property."

Inhale. Exhale. Continue. "Now your people have dug them up again. If there's danger, it's on their watch. But you don't think there is danger, because you went through your hazmat-and-walkie-talkie phase, and now you're here talking with me face to face."

"But what about the other four?" she glowered. "There were six crew positions, but only two bodies found. Are you harboring other aliens? Have they escaped?"

"Harboring aliens? As in illegal aliens? Not at all; they all had Green Cards! . . . . There were not another four." Oh, that was skirting the truth.

He spread his hands out as if to mollify me. "Young lady, I want to point out to you that there's evidence you have taken things away from this location, and we want to know who you have sold them to. They shouldn't fall into the wrong hands."

Calling me "young lady" did little to mollify me. "Evidence that I have taken things away? What evidence is that?"

"Obviously, it is not a complete vessel," he countered.

"What you see is what landed there. Where any other pieces are I have no idea. And what if I did take something? The law says if something falls onto my property from outer space, it belongs to me." I sat up straighter and thrust out my chest, and my lower lip.

She leaned toward me. "That will be for others to decide."

He also stood up taller. "We've found no means of propulsion, no fuel tanks, no defensive weapons. These are exactly the things that unnamed others would be most interested in."

She nodded agreement and crossed her arms. Good combative postures all around.

Now we were getting to their truth. I saw what their real interest was. "Ah, yes, I forgot. I got on the phone, called—who?—the Chinese? The North Koreans? Said I have an advanced propulsion system to sell you. And they came with their ships and helicopters and carried it away, all unseen. Is this your hypothesis?"

Thunderous frowns. They glanced at each other, as if hoping the other one would have a bright comeback.

"You're calling me a thief and a traitor with no evidence whatsoever."

Pursed lips and glowers, but they had nothing further to say. They'd been trying to intimidate me into admitting to heinous acts. Easy for me to fend off, since my crimes (if any) lay elsewhere.

"Something is preying on my mind. Am I going to get out of here alive?"

He seemed genuinely surprised at my question. She looked like she was seriously thinking it over.

"Unless you're planning to do me in and hide my body away, eventually your treatment of me will come to light. I'm not being treated in accordance with the Constitution of the United States. You haven't told me what I'm charged with; you haven't read me my rights. You have denied me the right to talk with anybody."

"For public health, and for national security purposes, we have the right to do that for a period of time," she intoned in her best Miranda voice.

"Bullshit! That time is over, if there ever was one." I shook my finger. "Get me my lawyer. Give me my call." I probably should have been nicer and meeker. Nice and meek are not my style in life. Would it have made a difference with them?

She turned away. "Well, technically, you're not under arrest, so those rules don't apply."

He also turned away. "This has helped a lot. But there are still some holes in the timeline we need to fill in. The sooner we do that, the sooner all this will be over."

They turned simultaneously and headed toward the door. "We'll be back to continue. Then you can contact your people. In the meantime, you're welcome to watch TV. We'll send up lunch shortly."

I always go to CNN for coverage of crises, and this was a crisis, for me anyway. Sure enough, a telephoto shot of my place from the air, taken from the north. There was my house, and holy shit, along the north edge of my property were several bulldozers and earthmovers carving a road of some sort, working up from Highway 1! They were halfway back to the crash site. I watched with mouth agape. Anger welled up in my throat. Helpless rage. No point to that; I just needed to calm down a bit.

Nice lunch, though. Tortilla salad, fish tacos, Coca Cola. Wherever we were, there must have been a decent Mexican deli nearby. But no cerveza, which I really needed. "Ooh, looky here," I giggled. "The name of the restaurant is on the taco wrapper!" Amigo Bueno. Downtown Oakland, right near City Hall. I once grabbed a bite there after a gig at the Rotunda. Maybe I was in the Courthouse. Did they have rooms like that for out-of-town witnesses or jurors? People who need to be "sequestered"?

In the desk drawer was a pad and pen, so I started keeping detailed notes on everything. I described my captors in detail. In my pique, I wrote, "Stacey = Stasi. Lew Spruce = Screw Loose."

Over the next few days, I was questioned and questioned and questioned. I can't claim they used "enhanced interrogation" on me, but it was sure boring after awhile. It's a good thing they didn't use a lie detector or some truth serum on me, because I was reluctant, shall we say, to reveal everything. I didn't exactly lie to them, but I didn't answer questions they didn't ask. Like my CPA advises me when talking to the IRS. But even the true parts were so flabbergasting, it was tough to sift out the inventions. I am a storyteller after all.

On Day—what? 4? 5? I asked in exasperation, "What is it you think I know or could tell you that you don't already know?"

"You haven't told us much so far," Screw Loose said, as if to a truculent child.

"And also, you're being held in quarantine, because of the whole microorganism factor," Smith asserted with her chin jutting out.

"Oh yeah? Well, you're not wearing white masks. You're going home at night. I think the quarantine story is baloney."

More fish tacos, more TV. I used my time to write all this up, even though I had no reason to believe they wouldn't take my notes away. If I had a window, I could train a pigeon to carry my notes to safety. If I could train a pigeon.

Your mind goes funny in these situations.

Here's why I don't watch much news on TV:

"Singer Selena Morisot, in a transparent effort to revive her flagging singing career, has concocted this story about a flying saucer landing on her property along the coast north of San Francisco. And now she has disappeared, and nobody will tell us where. Has she been abducted by her mysterious aliens? For who knows what purposes? We of course do not believe that for a moment. But those are the kinds of rumors swirling around."

Later, I got a helicopter-eye view of my spaceship being removed. I was royally pissed off but fascinated at the same time. They slid it down my hill across my property on the road they had constructed, using some kind of large sled, to Highway 1.

They leaked out various conflicting stories about what it was. A meth lab? A pot growing greenhouse? A dormitory for illegal aliens? (Little did they know how close they were!) The authorities tried to keep observers away, so much of the news footage was shot via telephoto lens by small planes and choppers circling high above, thus the jerky, off-focus quality.

To get the vessel across the highway, down the bluff, and onto a waiting barge, they had rigged up a pulley system on pylons, kind of like a downhill ski lift capable of hauling a locomotive. It looked like those contraptions they used along the coastline back in the 1800s to haul giant redwood logs out onto waiting boats. Environmental protection? Endangered species? Delicate shoreline? Feh! All was overlooked when the Feds decided to retrieve this hunk of off-world technology and study it for their own purposes.

I wondered why they didn't just haul it out with a huge helicopter. I found out. The spaceship must have been much heavier than they figured, because as they took it down over the steepest part of the bluff, one of the upper pylons collapsed, dumping the already-ruined vessel onto the steep slope, further damaging it. My poor spaceship! That of course happened live on worldwide TV.

What had happened to my friends and neighbors during all this? I was distraught to see on the news how they had been treated, knowing I had gotten them into the situation. They had all kept mum about Breadbox, as we had decided at the very beginning.

Sheriff Jim fared the worst. "Being an officer of the law, it cannot be excused that this happened on his watch," said some red-faced county official, flanked by four men who looked like G-men from central casting. He was put on administrative leave for failing to be aware of a potentially devastating public health crisis. The first confirmed contact with an alien space vessel, and initially he had claimed to know nothing about it. He was stoic and was assigned an excellent attorney, who limited any "fishing expedition" questions. So Jim answered each question tersely, but revealed no more than he had to.

His wife, Meg, I figured she'd be the one to blurt it all out and blow everybody's covers. But she came to the defense of her man in shrill, accusatory terms that turned her accusers' arguments and questions back on them.

"My husband is there to uphold the law, and the law says that when an object from space falls on private property, it belongs to that property owner, unless another owner comes forward. That did not happen in this case. So there was nothing for him to report."

Doc—my vet and Breadbox's dedicated caregiver, charter member of Sons of American Freedom, perpetually one step away from joining some hidden group in overthrowing the government—surprised me by coming across as a calm, reasoned defender of public health and safety.

"I examined two corpses of beings ostensibly from off this world. I am not qualified to draw a conclusion about that. I was obviously concerned they could pose a threat to public health. So we did two things. First, I did extensive testing of their blood and bodily fluids, to discover whether they harbored organisms that could spread a deadly pandemic. I worked with the most reputable and capable labs I know. We found no such organisms. Secondly, we decided the best course was to bury these bodies, in the off chance that there were organisms we failed to detect. In my judgment, this course of action was preferable to turning the corpses over to other authorities, which would require them to be moved through populous areas to be studied.

"I regret to say that in the aftermath of this situation, that is exactly what has happened. If any untoward events do transpire, in my opinion they will be due to the rash actions of those who moved them." He had this look on his face that said, finally, here's how I get back at "the Man."

"I stand behind my actions, and behind those of the property owner, Selena Morisot, and our local police authority, Sheriff James Osborne."

I cried when I heard him on TV. He was excellent! And I must confess, I'd been unaware that Doc had done so much testing. It wasn't till later that he showed me all his correspondence with the labs and their results. Since he certified they were not identifiable as human remains, he didn't have to identify who the test samples came from.

And Meg, bless her heart, kept going. "Those bastards pulled those poor beings out of the ground just like old-time grave robbers and took them off to who knows where. In the movies, it's Earth people being kidnapped by aliens and taken off for gruesome experiments. In this case, it's our own so-called leaders turning the tables and conducting their experiments on the aliens, I'm willing to bet."

Clay, my good friend, lawyered up and countered every question with another question. Here was his statement on CNN: "It comes down to this: we're in an area where there is little law and few precedents. We chose to proceed in one way. We could just as well have chosen differently. But nobody has shown that any laws were broken. And how else can ordinary citizens stand up against powerful and overweening government? Some feel the government is the ultimate arbiter on everything—and the ultimate protector. But if it is responsible for our protection in this situation, it has failed us utterly."

Even Dr. Allmon, the straight shooter who we figured would have notified the government, came to our defense. "While I would have handled this differently, and I'm sorry I wasn't called in, I won't gainsay the decision and actions of my fellow professionals."

How did I get out of quarantine? I learned afterwards that various people interceded on my behalf, including the ACLU—one of Doc's favorite nemeses. That kicked off a social media campaign that put a lot of pressure on somebody in the government. Dr. Screw Loose came in and said, "You're free to go! Mr. Jones here will take you home." Jones, Smith, whatever. Well, I don't use my real name either.

I was taken home to the wreckage of my garden and ransacked house. They had carved a new road along the side of my property back up the hill. Neighbor Jed told me that after they had backed a huge flatbed semi, plus a crane, it had taken them a few days to figure out how to retrieve the crashed vessel. I thought to myself that if I had gone to the county saying I wanted to build a road like that to the back of my property, it would have taken me five years to get the permits. And as a bonus, they bulldozed out most of the poison oak. The oak tree still stood over the whole scene.

I figured out afterwards that the main reason they kept me incommunicado for so long was to keep me away while they chopped up my property to retrieve the crashed vessel. As soon as it was removed, they took me home.

At sunset I took my favorite yard chair out back, sat there and just cried. I'd made a lot of mistakes in this escapade, and I was having big regrets. What if had I hastened the death of Breadbox, my best friend, by not getting her to a place where she would have received top-level treatment? Not taking anything away from Doc's level of care, but....

And the whole thing of ignoring the risk of diseases from other worlds. It turned out to be no big deal, but sheesh, we had no idea.

By keeping Breadbox secret, I hadn't been able to talk about her and tell people about her. I'd kept it all bottled up inside—so far. And this had been particularly tough with all the grilling I've gone through.

I couldn't get these thoughts out of my mind: I don't deserve to have her spaceship. I'm not worthy of it. I'm in way over my head in this whole affair. Whatever they do with it, they'll handle it much better than I could. Perhaps I should turn over the wand to them, so they can get the most out of it.

It was over. The whole episode was over. All that I'd worked for, my plans to return Breadbox to her home—first as a fully recovered being, then her remains—taken away without any discussion. Let alone compensation! Sadness and relief, and for missing Breadbox. Look, I'm a girl, I get to cry. I don't need any special reason!

Was their treatment of me legal? Depends on who you ask. Did I fight it afterwards? I must confess, I didn't. That's not what I wanted my life to be about. I had chosen to pour my passion into singing, not lawsuits. Plus, I could see that I had a bit of responsibility in the matter.

I checked to make sure Breadbox was still there, right where I had buried her in the artichoke patch. I dug down carefully to check. Yep, there she was. They had taken the two partners. Stasi said they had searched high and low for four others, but they never dug in my garden. And despite all the havoc, they hadn't yanked up my newly planted 'chokes.

I had also buried her wand, which she begged me to keep. I left Breadbox in peace but I retrieved the wand and brought it back to my house. I hid it under the loose floorboard, where the house's previous owner had stashed his dope. (I know this, because in his sudden departure, he'd left some pot behind. Pretty good stuff, too!)

At Sal's invitation, I went down to Locos Only on a Thursday evening. There was a line out to the street. Nothing like a performer with notoriety to fill a club to overflowing! Up on the stage, I sat on the stool, pulled the mike over, cradled Gibb and started singing. I am, after all, a singer.

> *Those alien blues*
> *They seem way too familiar to me…*

29. My 15 Minutes of Infamy

Does all the bad press get you down?
Still better than being ignored.
Do you draw scorn every walk to town?
Still better than being ignored.
From "Bad Press" on Inner-Galactic Journey album

I had felt a bit depressed when they brought me back to my home—and that was before I saw how they had ripped everything apart!

These people had taken Breadbox's spaceship—MY spaceship—without so much as a "thank you ma'am," let alone an offer of compensation. I feel like I've wimped out, helpless to do anything about it. What can I do to make amends to my friend? To let her clan know her fate, so they're not in ignorance forever?

But I had no time to feel sorry for myself, because the news industry hit me like a swarm. It lasted through the holiday season—the dark months of the year.

Out of the frying pan, into the fire, to coin a cliché. Out of detention, into the maelstrom of mainstream media. I had always been a glutton for publicity, and I sure got my fill of it over the next couple of months. Alas, not the kind I really like. But you know what they say: Good publicity, bad publicity, doesn't matter, so long as your name's getting out there. I got my fifteen minutes of fame, notoriety, ridicule, whatever.

The interviews and stories have ranged from sublime to ridiculous. I'll share a few of them, starting with the ridiculous.

But first, the one thing that pissed me off the most. Some toy company came out with action figures for the holiday season, based on the reconstructed remains of the dead crew members and the spaceship and I didn't even get a cut of it! Not a cent! "Why should you be paid?" one of their attorneys asked me. "Because these were taken from my property!" It was obvious to me. I need better lawyers.

The Enquirer, The Star, even CNN piled on. My favorite headline: "Giant Artichokes That Glow in the Dark. The aliens' secrets of fertilization could make world hunger disappear!" With a blown-up, Photoshopped picture of my tiny 'chokes.

And speaking of fertilization…

"Alien Love Baby. Soon to make a debut?" with my frazzled, frumpy frame on the cover. The evidence? Well, I hadn't denied it, so it must be true. After all, isn't that what happens with aliens in flying saucers and Earth women?

They'd come onto my property to interview me in my pre-coffee hour, the morning after a gig, when I wasn't looking or feeling my best. I growled, "Do I look pregnant to you? Those days are past, folks." The guy was sticking the TV camera obtrusively in my face, so I stumbled against him and "accidentally" yanked the cable out of the jack, making sure I bent it. A woman poked at my garden with a spade that was leaning against the fence, fiddling with the artichokes. Whoa, too close to my friend beneath the roots! "Leave my garden alone," I yelled. I grabbed the shovel from her. I'm truly sorry it swung around and smacked her in the shin. Maybe that accounts for the lousy cover photo.

I kinda brought it on myself, because to keep my sanity, I did some, shall we say, tongue-in-cheek interviews. Here's the one you probably saw on TV. I was in the studio in San Francisco, being interviewed by several reporters who were at least as profound as the alien love baby crowd. They asked silly questions, so I answered them in kind.

Reporter 1: "Selena. That means 'of the Moon.' Do you claim to be a Moon maiden?"

"Not really. My parents are from France, though. They knew the Coneheads."

Reporter 2: "What did our cosmic visitors do for recreation while they were here?"

Me: "They went to casinos to gamble. They won big! Strangely, nobody recognized them. I taught them to play poker. But they loved playing Twister. They were unbeatable, because of their long limbs and tentacles. We should never have played Strip Twister though."

Reporter 3: "I've been wondering—we've all been wondering—why did the aliens even want to visit Earth?"

Me: "They've left now, for good. They had hoped to save us, but found that we are beyond redemption.

"They wanted to learn from us, but then wondered what we could teach them. They wanted to teach us, but no one would listen. We only listen to the wrong things.

"They wanted to have a quiet sit-down with our leaders, to see if our world is ready to join the galactic community. But our leaders fought amongst themselves for the right to sit next to the aliens.

"Then they thought maybe they'd just conquer us, but things here are so chaotic, they saw we couldn't be conquered. So they gave up and went back home. It's probably for the best, don't you agree?"

This last bit is the clip that has been played and replayed and forwarded so many times! I regret it, for the ruckus it caused, but I can't help but chuckle. Most people, hopefully my fans and readers among them, saw it as a spoof. But some believed every word, like it was gospel!

Each of my statements seemed to have an interest group out there, and they all sent their kooky lobbyists to argue with me afterward.

"Aliens have been here—for thousands of years. Most of our great teachings come from them. Do you think it's a coincidence that several of the world's great religions all got their start at around the same time?"

"They've slowly been conquering us by interbreeding and dumbing down our species." That I could just about believe. It didn't say much for the smarts of the alien race, though.

"I have traveled to the galactic councils, so don't mock them. It is so beautiful, so transcendent. Tall, thin, ethereal beings in white robes." Sounded like a secular version of Heaven.

"I'm one of the few who was taken aboard their spaceship, and I have the alien love child, as you call it, to prove it. My boy Herald was sent back to bring their message of wisdom." Herald was a funny-looking little kid, with a weak chin and huge ears, ratty hair, but no little alien antennas. I was thinking more Neanderthal.

I should have had a tee shirt made: "We who have cavorted with aliens get annoyed by you who only claim you have."

My irreverent reactions made some people quite angry at me, to the point where I was concerned for my safety. I got threats. I'd never before felt the full brunt of the hatred of anonymous social media flamers. After I moved up here from LA, I semi-retired from Twitter and Facebook and all that. Now I had to withdraw completely, but other people would keep me informed of the vile stuff coming my way. Sheriff Jim became my de facto bodyguard, despite the trouble I had caused for him.

"But they took the spaceship from me," I protested online. "It's out of my hands now. No point in hounding me." To which I got three different responses:

"Why didn't you turn it over to the authorities sooner?" or

"Why did you ever turn it over?" or

"Where have you hidden it?"

Fortunately, their fire flamed high but soon burned itself out. It subsided to occasional harassment from the tabloids.

I guess I overrate people's sense of humor. An example: After my detention, I assumed "they" (government? press?) were tapping my phone, cell, email—everything. To test that theory, I phoned Clay and said that I would be traveling late that evening to the Mother Ship that would be hovering over Ames, Iowa at dawn. Sure enough, the blogosphere reported that at dawn the next day in Ames, several black SUVs with tinted windows surreptitiously showed up and drove around. Government? Or media? I don't know.

The guy I hired to survey my house for bugs, no surprise, found a few. But he couldn't guarantee there weren't more sophisticated ones tucked away.

Did I tell you I got a new agent? Not my musician's agent Morty, bless his tone-deaf soul, but one worthy of a semi-big celebrity with skeletons to keep hidden, and media pounding on my door. I was spending so much time being interviewed for free I couldn't get any work done, so I decided to start charging the media vultures and paparazzi.

And still people called, or just dropped by unannounced. Those who said they had been on flying saucers, had travelled to the stars, and wanted to share stories with me.

It wasn't all like that. PBS News Hour did a segment on me. I've always dreamed of being invited onto that program for my music, but oh well, I took what I could get.

News Hour: "Today we are fortunate to have Selena Morisot, whose music I have long enjoyed. Selena, welcome!

NH. "You've been a composer and singer of some renown." I never get tired of hearing that. Maybe someday I'll come to believe it. "But lately you've been thrust into the news because of a space vessel that crash landed on your farm in Northern California."

"Yes. And please let me apologize to your viewers for all the non-serious interviews I have been involved in."

NH. "How has this experience changed your life?"

"It's too soon to tell. Invite me back in a year and ask me. I'm still caught up in the flurry of interviews and questions from the authorities. Little time for reflection yet. It hasn't really sunk in with me.

NH. "Nor with the rest of us, I think it's safe to say. Here is the first undeniable evidence of intelligent life from outside the Earth. This will have an unimaginable impact on us over years to come.

"I agree. It's kind of like the stages of grief that we haven't come to grips with yet. I think people are still in the stage of denial about this. All these people who are interviewing me about alien love children and other silly things are just not able to comprehend the likely impact."

NH. "Don't you think it will have a positive impact on our technology?

"Sure, scientists will discover all kinds of things from that spaceship that will turn out to be of great benefit to humankind. But it could also lead to huge problems. What if governments fight over it? Or it benefits some more than others? Or we discover new ways to kill or subjugate each other? It's too soon to tell."

NH. "Won't the knowledge that there are other intelligent beings help draw us together? Just knowing that we're not alone?"

"I would sure hope so. But we've never been alone, even here in this world. We've always had each other, yet we call each other alien. If we make the aliens out to be enemies, then maybe it will draw us together. But that would be the wrong outcome. I think we need to learn to view them, and ourselves, with more love. And interest. If we use knowledge of them to learn more about ourselves, that will be valuable."

NH. "What about you personally?"

"This is so hard for me to answer, this soon. There are many things in the universe that can touch our hearts and souls. We have to be open. I'm trying to remain open.

"This experience brings all the clichés to life. Do what is most important and meaningful to yourself, because life is precious and fleeting. Follow your passion. As crazy as it might sound, this has inspired me to write songs from my heart and soul, to worry less about what will sell and be popular."

What I was dying to say, but couldn't, was, "I made the best friend I've ever had in my life. She was this funny-looking little alien. She opened me up to so many things, both out there but also in my own soul. Then she died. I am devastated and heartbroken."

Why couldn't I tell the world? Well, if I did, then I'd have to tell what happened to her and where the body was buried. They would dig her up. I don't know for sure what they did with the bodies of her crewmembers, but I'm willing to bet it involved cutting them up and conducting experiments on them. I mean, hell, isn't this exactly the boogieman tale about what the nasty aliens do to us when they abduct us?

Some wanted so much for the report of the alien visit to be true. Others were scared it was true. Some took it seriously, like the News Hour crew. And yet others—especially in the media—played it as a game, to drive ratings with sensational stories.

A professional debunker, some professor whose name I've already blanked out, came to interview me so he could pick my story apart and expose me as a fraud. He had a young grad student with him. He had no trouble picking my story apart—both the true parts and the lies. I neglected to tell him about Breadbox under the artichokes—or about the wand right under the easy chair he was sitting in, or about the amulet on a chain around my neck. He was so smug and arrogant. He used the old Sherlock Holmes line: When everything else is eliminated, what remains must be true. Since interstellar travel was impossible, it had to be a hoax, and I had to be a charlatan. Perhaps the government was in league with me. I rocked in my rocker and hummed, "Whatcha gonna believe—me or your lyin' eyes?"

The grad student, Dana, was very interested, though. She took exactly the opposite viewpoint. "Something is happening here. We need to pay attention. Let's gather data, even anecdotes, before we make judgments."

He was having none of it, and he gave her a dirty look. "Perhaps we're done here," he said, getting up. "May I use your bathroom?"

"Sure. Watch out for the alien who lives in the toilet!" His assistant tried to stifle her laughter and ended up snorting.

Dana said to me in a hushed voice, so El Professor wouldn't overhear, "Could I follow up with you? Just kind of keep in touch as things unfold? I don't think we can trust the government to tell us everything. I'd much rather have direct contact with you."

"I would be delighted." Here, I thought, was a kindred spirit. "But… why do you take me seriously?" We exchanged cards. I wrote my new, secret email address on the back for her.

"When confronted with strong evidence of the impossible, it's time to change your thinking, even if you can't explain it. So many of these stories fall apart at the first touch. But this one, we keep poking it, and it pokes back."

Those two offered the perfect example of what they mean when they say knowledge advances one funeral at a time. The tenured keepers of the orthodoxy must die before there's space for new ideas to emerge and be taken seriously.

"And I must admit," she said as she put away her notebook, "I would sure love it to be true."

*   *   *

By late December the hubbub had pretty much died down, as people turned their attention to after-Christmas sales. The aliens hadn't invaded. No worldwide pandemic. A hurricane in the Caribbean monopolized the headlines. The New York Times ran occasional articles on the results of studies on the confiscated vessel and alien bodies. They were so bland you knew the poobahs were trying to conceal their discoveries.

I was so glad to hang out in my little home on the coast, sit on the deck—even during the winter storms—and sip chardonnay with my friends. I talked with Breadbox, still alive in my spirit, and kept up a running dialogue of all the silly things that were happening here.

Wow, did I ever have a creative burst of songwriting those next few weeks, as the days grew longer in the new year! This time I did not hold back. I poured heart and soul into all my formerly private songs. That's when I wrote "Space Girl Yearning" about Breadbox's dilemma of choosing. I put as much of her in there as I could without quite being explicit about my visitor. Also "Anthem for My Secret Self" and "Agate"— both of which went to #1, as you probably know.

30 Home Phoned

When Impossibility calls your name,
You better listen up
From Inner-Galactic Journey album by Selena Morisot

Have you ever lost a digital watch? Every day at the same time, you hear the faint beep of its alarm. You try to find it in the twenty seconds before the beeping stops. I was having that experience, but I'd lost no watch, so what was beeping? When it was very quiet I would sometimes hear this faint "deedle deedle deedle." Sometimes it sounded like a tiny muffled voice. But I couldn't figure out where it was coming from.

One night, I dreamed of Breadbox's mother looking for her and calling her name, even though Breadbox had explained that she didn't really have a mother. But I got it; that was it! It was the wand, hidden beneath my floorboards, covered by an area rug and a rocking chair. I got it out. Silent and inert. I left it beside my bed, wrapped in a towel to hide it from casual spies.

Next day I was in the garden doing some early-spring weeding and heard it through the bedroom window. I ran in to see what it was doing. A dim light pulsed on its side. I pushed at the light as if it were a button. "What does this thing do?" I muttered. Visions of ET phoning home. It chirped at me—a tinny, broken sound, or series of sounds. Clearly it was responding to me. Sounded like communication. I had heard the wand speak many times, and this sounded very different, as if it was channeling a ghost.

What to say? "Son of a bitch!" I responded thoughtfully. That was my greeting to the cosmos. I picked up the wand, flung it onto my bed, and covered it with my pillow and held it down, as if trying to smother an intruder. I could still hear its muffled chirp.

All our devices and appliances talk to us; why should this surprise me? Was it the gizmo itself, or was it conveying a message from across deep space?

I uncovered it and picked it up, gazing at it like the ape in the movie "2001" looking at the obelisk. Just a plain-looking gray cylinder, a bit over a foot long. Then it blew a bubble, like with bubble gum.

Was this wand "it" or "she?" I'd already forgotten that the wand was

Wanda, and a "she," not an "it." Out of sight, out of mind.

I lay Wanda the Wand on her side on my bed. A space resembling a translucent bubble the size of a large beach ball grew above her. It was as if I was looking into a hole. Things inside there popped and swirled. It was mesmerizing. The patterns of light and sound echoed and roared. Lots of movement and racket for such a small—and imaginary—space. I thought I was gazing into the maw of infinity. It was hard to look at, it hurt my eyes and ears, but I couldn't look away. Indeed, I drew closer, to get a better view of the impossible patterns. It reminded me of what you see on an LSD trip. I had to restrain myself from sticking my hand in there, for fear I could not pull it out. I could get totally sucked into that space, and then where would I be?

A symbol popped into the space, a rotating cube. It seemed to suck up the cacophony of sound, and turn it into a soft hum, actually a simple chord. I could dupe that on Gibb. The cube appeared to have three-dimensional solidity, even though transparent, like a cube of glass. As it rotated, each face seemed to have other cubes attached like ghosts, and they twisted around in impossible ways. It reminded me of the time, when I was a kid, my dad showed me how to draw a four-dimensional cube—a tesseract—on paper, and I actually constructed one with toothpicks and chewing gum.

In the center of each square face was a faint symbol, which quickly rotated past. Each one seemed different. Reminded me of the ancient Sanskrit writing you see in Buddhist prayers.

Then the cube faded and slid to the side of the bubble, to be replaced by a visage, bright blue and red and violet pulsing colors. I couldn't tell if it was a live being of some sort, or a robot or device. But it spoke, in a staticky, slurring voice, quite rapid, but monotone. Its "mouth" moved. Its two eyes, which were next to its mouth, darted this way and that, independently. It sounded like a loud voice in a large echoing room. It would speak, then pause, then speak again. Like it was saying the same thing over and over. I was startled to hear Wanda's softer, well-modulated voice, closer at hand, speaking English to me, apparently translating. That's her job. "Contactee is not recognized. Registered users, please reveal."

It then faded and was replaced by another image. Dark blue and feather-covered, looked like Oscar the Grouch with a gold beak, but the sharp beak of an octopus. A deep, raspy squawk. Looked and sounded officious. A cop! What had I done? I surmised it was because I was using the personal instrument of Breadbox and her friends.

Wanda explained to me that this entity wanted to see Breadbox or one of the other crewmembers. Alas. Wanda "spoke" into this space in her beedle-boop mode I had heard with Breadbox. Then she translated herself to me: "Registered users not available. Serious Level 1 occurrence. Alternate rules must apply. Viewed contactee is the senior oki available."

This quieted things for a moment. But it quickly became the conference call from heaven and hell. "Heaven" because it was happening at all. To all indications, I was in contact with a location somewhere across the cosmos—i.e., the heavens. It was 3-D; it looked like I could jump in. It was magic come to life! "Hell" because this space was soon filled by a host of jabbering entities, all hooting and squawking and clicking and rasping at the same time.

Wanda sounds like the voice your car uses when it gives you directions. Smooth, excellent diction, no emotion. Just the opposite of the raucous cacophony issuing from the bubble projecting from her.

The image of the entity filling the space drew back, revealing a host of others—all looking completely different. One looked a bit like Breadbox. At first I thought they were ranged around the edge of a room, but then I saw that each one appeared to be in a separate place, but places with similar backgrounds, so that their images were stitched together into a single "room." Some were crisp and sharp and steady, with bright colors; others were a bit muddy and blurry, and their images vibrated and jerked a bit.

Wanda translated snatches of this cacophony, but it was like getting a translation of everybody at a cocktail party jabbering at once.

Finally I had the nerve to say something. "I am known as Agate, friend of Breadbox." All stopped jabbering. Wanda beedle-booped, presumably translating.

Purple face moved back in to dominate the space and growled a monotone ditty several times. Then the spinning cubes returned, and then the connection was broken. Wow, did they just hang up on me?

Selena speaks with aliens using Wanda

Wanda explained, "They do not recognize you as a being with whom they can communicate. They demand to see the crewmembers. When they hear that this is impossible, they want to communicate only with Wanda. They ask questions about you and the crew. Wanda informs them that you are senior oki present. Yet they do not accept that. They order us to produce the crew. They will reconnect in a given time period—a portion of a day here."

*   *   *

Late that night I once again heard the tiny deedle-deedle signal. The bubble formed above Wanda, containing the image of the rotating four-dimensional cubes, quickly fading to the "room" crowded with images of diverse aliens. I hadn't counted, but it looked like there were several new ones this time. Once again, it was cacophony. Many voices echoing in background, like on an old phone party line. Wanda struggled to translate for me. Snatches of speech, but not entire statements. They were talking about me, but not to me.

They wanted to talk to Wanda and ignore me, but Wanda said to me, "Internal rules say it is not proper for Wanda, a device, to answer for you, an oki. So their questions shall be conveyed to you for you to answer, then Wanda will respond using your answers."

The questions poured forth. "What happened to our clan son and daughters? Have they been killed? Eaten? What is this barbarian whose visage appears? How did it acquire their private device? Where are you? How did the vessel get there?"

Through Wanda, I answered as best I could, even the ones about the primitive barbarian who may have eaten their compatriots. It was troubling to me that it would even occur to them that I, a being with whom they were conversing, might eat their compatriots. What did this say about them? Did Wanda perhaps mis-translate, or I mis-hear?

After a time, we gave up the pretense that Wanda was answering independently, and they started addressing me directly.

As the evening wore on, some left, so at least half the beings remaining were of the same species as Breadbox. Which ones might be her closest kin? I tried to imagine that I was speaking to Breadbox's mother, or at least some being who cared for her that much. I related the entire story. I saw no reason to hold back. I explained the fate of the other two travelers, then talked in great detail about Breadbox and my interactions with her. I spoke slowly and allowed Wanda to translate—hoping they could understand reasonably well.

As we went on, the beings in the bubble listened attentively as Wanda conveyed my explanations and rarely interrupted, asking a few clarifying questions.

Wanda had to answer their question about how they got here, and it caused a further uproar. "The crew discovered jump codes to worlds that

141

lie outside the Confederation. The vessel travelled to several such worlds, and unfortunately, came to a mishap on one—this one."

The others were outhooted by Mr. Rooster: "What you relate to us is impossible. It cannot happen. If you refuse to give us an accurate account. . . If you tell us these false tales . . . ." He didn't seem to know how to complete his threat. What exactly would he do if he could?

I worked in a few questions of my own. Who were they? Who was Breadbox-Nala really? Where were they? How had Breadbox travelled here? And were they coming after her?

I was amazed to learn that, even though we were communicating in real time (whatever the hell that means in this context) they had no idea where I was, and couldn't explain where they were in relation to me. If they were to be believed, this meant they weren't coming here to pick up the remains.

All were by now speaking calmly, except Mr. Rooster. "It is appalling, it is without precedent, that one of our many-purposed controller and communication devices would fall into the hands of a primitive non-oki from outside the Galactic Confederation of All Oxygen Worlds. This is a catastrophe of unknowable proportions and consequences! We must repair this breach!" It sounded like he was ready to leap through the ether to retrieve Wanda.

This back and forth lasted far into the wee hours, with some of them leaving the connection. My bedside clock said it was after 4 am when we had finally asked and answered all our questions, some multiple times. We fell silent and regarded each other. Three sapient squids, an officious bird, and a hairless ape. Across an impossible abyss—yet in a way, so familiar.

The others' images winked off one by one leaving only the officious Mr. Rooster, clicking impotently. Then his image was replaced by the rotating cubes. I was about to turn away when one image returned—one of the beings of Breadbox's world. She sang a phrase to Wanda, and I was astounded that I could understand her directly.

"Permission to speak to the contactee?" she trilled.

With my two index fingers, I did my best to duplicate the tentacle twirl of assent I had learned from Breadbox.

"I am Kateh, clan mother to Nala." She trilled and thrummed, and Wanda translated.

"I am Agate, friend of Nala. I am honored that you will speak with me." I responded in English. Wanda spoke the language I had come to recognize as Fedi. "Your clan daughter became a dear friend to me in the short time she was here. I am so sorry the other two crewmembers perished in the crash. I did my utmost to care for Nala, with the hope that she could return to your world. We taught each other many things about our worlds. Her death was unexpected, but I will honor her memory my entire life."

"I am distraught with my sense of loss," she crooned. "Yet I must be angry for the taboo actions taken by our young clan members. I suspect that Nala was not the leader. There's a reason such activity is proscribed for our people. They failed, as was inevitable."

"They were a team. They collaborated closely," I said to her, wanting to head off the notion that Breadbox had been victimized by the others. "Nala and Alala and Novan set out to discover interesting and valuable new worlds beyond your Confederation. They did this in secret because it went against your rules. Nala told me that they could not return home unless they had evidence of an interesting world that they had discovered.

"I am that evidence," I asserted strongly. "I want you to know that they fulfilled their mission. They discovered an advanced, high-technology world that lies outside your known circle of worlds. My world. If they hadn't, you and I could not be having this conversation. They broke your rules, but they deserve your pride, and your accolades. Their loss is your sorrow, but their discovery is worthy of the ancient heroes of your people."

By holding my phone up to Wanda, I showed photos of Breadbox and played some recorded singing.

She was visibly moved by these, and was then silent a while. "You must understand, the things you have told me frighten those with more authority and wisdom than I. They don't want contact with those like you."

"For fear of what?"

"Challenging the established order. Awakening ancient ghosts that caused so much turmoil in our past. If all our would-be explorers were out making contact with worlds like yours . . ." She trailed off.

She thanked me for the care I had given. It was truly in the highest tradition of oki of me, she said.

I was about to say I was signing off, but asked one final question: "If possible, would you like me to return the remains of your clan members to your world?"

"Alas, alas, it is not possible," was her muddled message back to me. "But we were pleased to learn their story."

I sat on the edge of my bed and trembled for maybe half an hour at the enormity of what had just transpired. How does one come to terms with carrying on a conversation across such a void? These beings were so unlike me, and yet just like me—or people I have known. And nobody would believe me that it had happened. Unless Wanda had recorded the interchange. Hmm. I decided to ask her in the morning.

Okay, I've been calling Wanda "her." A gizmo. Clearly nothing female about it except the name I had bestowed. If this device is something I carry on conversations with all the time, it's hard to think of it as an "it"— even though it's a dull-gray metallic thing. Wanda's voice was a version of mine—except it came off kind of unisex. She has no personality. Just a mechanism that talks, like our phones and our cars. So you see I switch back and forth between "she" and "it." We'll see. Maybe I'll put some lipstick on her. Make a little smiley face.

*　　*　　*

There was an interesting postscript to this contact. In summarizing what had transpired, Wanda reported to me that before they signed off, the beings we were communicating with had ordered it to destroy itself. This presented a dilemma to its little robot mind. Its first rules are, don't allow oki to be damaged by its actions or decisions, and secondly, don't destroy information. Since it had loaded up with so much information about Earth and English, self-destruction would violate the second rule. In such cases, it informed me, it was taught to ask its controlling oki to suggest the best course. It wanted my opinion: did I think it should destroy itself?

"Well, no I don't. Not at all! And what's this about me being the 'controlling oki?'"

Wanda explained her reasoning. "All the crew members are gone. The last remaining crew member—Nala/Breadbox—told Wanda to teach you, Agate, and to follow your instructions in case Breadbox oki was not available." The beings with whom we had communicated on its home world had decided not to have it return home. They were abandoning it. Thus, Wanda had deduced that I was now the controlling oki.

The most powerful gadget I had ever imagined was now my faithful sidekick. But I discovered I was holding a grudge against this metallic helper. I had to ask, "Before Breadbox died, didn't you know her condition?" Sure, blame it on the machine.

"Wanda is sorry to say, our friend neglected to connect the sensors monitoring her health, so Wanda could not know of her impending death. Deduced that she did not want me to know." Hmm. That's twice that Wanda didn't or couldn't prevent dire consequences because she was left out of the loop.

I couldn't understand why Wanda was so reluctant to refer to herself as "I" or "me." Like she thought it improper. Well, I didn't want to refer to her as "it" either, so we each had our peculiarities about this. Interesting that a metallic cylinder can have preferences and scruples and idiosyncrasies.

"Wanda, as the controlling oki, I give you permission, when you are speaking to me, to refer to yourself as 'I,' as if you are a sapient being—an oki. This is for convenience of communication. Is this okay? Can you do this?"

"Yes, Wanda can do that. I can."

So, of course, I then had to explain the difference between "I" and "me"—dredging up my junior-high grammar.

Later, it turned out there was a post-postscript as well. Wanda informed me that sometime after this episode, a data pill had appeared in her message chain. It was the private direct-contact code for Kateh, the clan mother of Breadbox. It was in the form of a small snatch of melody. It will be the first number in my brand-new cosmic phone book.

Could I build a song around it?

There I sat, waiting for dawn. In my simple, back-country, guitar-strumming, cowgirl way, I had suddenly come into control of this device that put me in touch with the whole wide universe. If what Breadbox told me was true, then with this amulet I had greater reach than the most powerful beings in her Galactic Confederation. No wonder Mr. Rooster was upset!

31. I Want My Spaceship Back!

> *Yes, the man is a bully*
> *Just what can I do?*
> *Well, if he don't stop me*
> *I'll sing out for my spaceship,*
> *I'll sing out for you.*
>> From "My Spaceship Calls Out to Me"
>> on Inner-Galactic Journey album

"I want my spaceship back!" I demanded loudly. I actually pounded my fist on the table. He stroked his scraggly beard and looked at me calmly.

"The government came onto my land without my permission, took things that were my property, and also took me into custody without justification!" I was getting worked up. It really pisses me off when someone I'm yelling at remains calm and unperturbed.

I'd spotted him right away when he came to my singing gig at Locos Only. He was the only one sitting calmly during my raucous follow-up to "Space Girl Yearning." He was the only one with a corduroy jacket and yellow socks. "Calmly" I've said several times now. That's him. Calm. Even when the stuff hits the fan.

I knew that he would stick around after my set and come talk with me. He had the look. I didn't get at first that he was a government functionary. He didn't have that look. "Just call me Ed," he told me, as we pulled a small bistro table and chairs over into a quieter corner. He said he was an astrophysicist who had been brought in by the government to study the vessel after it was taken into custody by the Feds. He was "retired" (looked way too young to be retired) from government service. Thus, as he explained, he took no position on whether the "artifact"—as he called it—should have been taken.

"Ditzy chick," he smirked. "That's what they call you, you know. Surely you want to prove them wrong."

"I've been called worse."

"We found six harnesses. You buried two bodies. So there must be four more aliens somewhere. Dead? Alive? I saw those bodies. They weren't made for running. So they were moved—dead or alive."

"Your buddies grilled me for days on that question. There's no team of aliens skulking around in the hills."

"I know you know much more than you've said. Don't deny it or admit it. Just hear me out."

I leaned back in "hear him out" mode, arms folded across my chest.

"Let me tell you a story. Once upon a time a young girl stumbled across something beautiful and enticing and valuable. It wasn't actually hers, and she had no idea of its real worth, yet she took a few baubles away as souvenirs."

"Good story. Now it's my turn. Once upon a time, a bunch of powerful men came onto this lone woman's farm—woman, not a girl!—and took something valuable from her that did not belong to them. They did this because they could, even though they cloaked their action in lots of high-flown justifications. They wrapped themselves in the authority of "The Man," and professed to act for the public good. But then everything ended up being under their control, and for their benefit. I could write a song about that. It would go right to the top of the charts."

He sat there unfazed.

I took a deep breath and went on. "Who owns this thing, anyway? Why does it not belong to me? "

He leaned forward. "I knew it. You wanted to keep all this to yourself, to make yourself rich and famous."

"I'm already rich and famous—enough for me anyway."

"Maybe you thought you could help mankind."

"That's 'humankind.' That would be admirable of me. So why was I not doing anything with it?"

"Why would I believe that's true? I figure you are doing something with it."

"I don't even have it any more! You have it."

"I mean the pieces you removed."

"But you see no evidence of that, even though you're undoubtedly tapping my phone and reading my emails and all my internet doings. Must be boring duty for you or your minions. I'd like to ask what YOU and your buddies are doing with it."

I jabbed my finger at him. "And . . . I have no idea who you are, except you say your name is Ed, and you wear yellow socks."

He handed me his card, which said very little:

EDWIN X. HU, PHD
ASTROPHYSICS

Plus cell phone and email address. It was Gmail. Maybe he really was retired.

"You're Doctor Who!" I giggled, drawing out the who-o-o. "Where's your coat and long scarf?"

"That's not original," he humphed.

"You're trying to build your own tardis, aren't you?" I continued, leaning toward him like Perry Mason with a hostile witness.

He leaned away from me. "Hardly. We're putting it to proper scientific study. By the best people, I assure you."

I sat back and roared with laughter. "Ha, ha, ha! Just like that bit from the end of 'Raiders of the Lost Ark.' 'We have top men working on this.' 'Who?' 'Top. Men.' You remind me so much of that government functionary talking to Indiana Jones when you said that."

Dr. Hu was offended by this, so I continued to dig. "You're dissecting those poor aliens, to learn what makes them tick. You're looking for technologies to exploit—to make yourselves rich. To gain military advantage. You'd like to figure out how to fly to the stars. Under an American flag, of course."

He slowly regained his air of calm and regarded me professorially. I swear he did a bit of yoga breathing. "Well, that's the rub. There are key pieces missing, even though we've scoured your property and the surrounding area, and the ocean bottom. We dredged up one major piece from off shore. It's part of the propulsion system apparently. But no thrusters, no fuel tanks. We can't figure out what makes it go. So I decided to come have a further chat with you to see if you could help."

Yeah, he wanted my help. So he had to make nice with me no matter how bratty I was. Notice, he hadn't denied my contentions.

"I didn't know you'd found more pieces. Where are you keeping it . . . if that's not secret. Area 51 in Nevada?"

"Very funny. Actually, Edwards Air Force Base in the Mojave."

"The Mojave, eh? I'm curious. How do you move something like this—bound to attract big attention—from my backyard to the distant desert?"

"So, we took it offshore right from your place and put it on a large barge, as you probably know." He enjoyed the cleverness of it all. "Towed the barge down to Pendleton—the Marine station. Put it on a big flatbed there, covered in tarps, and made a slow 3 am run up I-15 across the Cajon Pass. Into a secure hangar in a place that's already crawling with derelict aircraft. Nobody knew it happened. Nobody in the press, anyway."

I tried to envision derelict aircraft crawling around, zombie-like. I must confess, he actually seemed to be telling the truth. That's when you need to be on your guard with these guys.

He was quiet for a minute. "It's trying to repair itself!"

"What?" I almost yelled. "How is it doing that?"

"I was hoping you could shed some light," he pled.

I scoffed. "How the hell would I know? You're telling me things I was totally unaware of. I'm afraid I really am the ditzy chick here."

That stopped the conversation for a moment. Then I asked, "How big is it, once you get the pieces together?"

"Like the fuselage of a small commuter jet. Ten feet across, maybe seventy long—if we had all the pieces."

"So what do you mean, it's fixing itself?"

He resumed the professor mien. "It's strange. Talk about a technology we'd like to understand! The metal grows slowly, like a plant. At first we thought our measurements were screwy, but we put a time-lapse camera on it. And that showed clearly it was growing metal to cover the damaged gaps. Until the camera stopped working. And that's the strangest part! It seems like it draws material from surrounding things to create its own repairs."

"That is totally amazing! It ate your camera?"

"Enough so it stopped working. So, we moved some old airliners into the hangar with it so it would have something to feed on."

"Ah, yes, let the hungry alien feed on its own kind." I said conspiratorially.

He ignored this. "We've tested small samples of its fuselage so we know what kind of materials it needs. Mostly aluminum, titanium, and some kind of complex polymer or ceramic we haven't fully analyzed yet. We noticed that after we remove a tiny sample, it "heals" itself and grows back! When we examine it under a microscope, you know what it's closest to? Wood! Like fine ceramic, metallic wood.

"Well, wood is made to grow. That must make your mouth water. So, then, what are you going to do after it rebuilds itself?"

"We figure it will attract a pilot eventually. Some being who knows how to fly it. Someone we'd dearly love to talk to."

"Aha!" I snorted. "And who knows? If I happen to know where these mystery alien pilots are hiding out, perhaps they'll get the word. Well, hopefully they're studying up on English while they're lurking about." After a pause. "I assure you, if there are other aliens, I know nothing about them."

He looked down at his watch, seemingly disappointed that I couldn't lead him to the Captain Kirk of the aliens.

"Oh, by the way, have you figured out where it came from?"

Suddenly he got animated. "No. Nor how it got here. Obviously, it came from beyond our solar system. Knowing that it traveled between stars gets our scientists' minds going. This tin can doesn't look capable of traveling to Mars, let alone Tau Ceti or wherever. They must have traveled in suspended animation. But it doesn't seem outfitted for that."

"No warp drive, then?" I asked innocently.

He looked like he was dying to say more, but held his tongue. So I continued.

"Let me ask you a question. Even if your 'top men' can't figure out how it works, I mean, if they deduce that the only thing that makes sense, given the facts you have, is that it somehow traveled faster than the speed of light, how would they react?

"Oh, they'll deny it and rage against it!" He rubbed his hands together with glee at the prospect. It was the first glimmer of liking I had for him.

He explained what I—a mere woman and rock singer—had thought myself. "If empirical facts are discovered that contradict your theories, then your theories have to change. I've been going back and re-examining all the equations from relativity and quantum physics, and there are these terms tucked away in there, or possible solutions of the equations, that were always neglected because they seemed to make no sense. Could a warp drive be hidden in there? Facts on the ground trump theories in textbooks. If the facts have been interpreted correctly. We're still a long ways from concluding that."

Somehow it slipped my mind to tell him that I had carried on extended conversations with beings across the cosmos using Wanda the Wand—in ways that totally violated Dr. Hu's astrophysics. And that of his "top men."

Yes, I did have the missing pieces of course, but I thought, I'll be damned if I'm handing them over to this guy, or to anyone else.

Even during this discussion I was wearing the amulet, as I had been since the death of Breadbox. Probably the most valuable piece of metal in the known universe, from what Breadbox had told me. And he had no idea.

I had been working with Wanda almost every night, exploring all the hidden nooks of information and instructions, with the glee of a kid in a candy store. She was eager to divulge the innermost secrets she contained. She remembered how to get to Earth, and how to get home. She knew how to translate all the codes contained in the amulet that could allow the vessel to jump to worlds throughout this part of the galaxy.

The implications of what Dr. Hu told me didn't fully hit home till 2:30 the next morning. Suddenly I was wide awake. Breadbox gave up hope when she realized her vessel could never return home. Now these men, through sheer doggedness—and huge taxpayer-funded expense—had dredged and dragged and kluged all the pieces back together. Gotten them close enough together, and with needed raw materials nearby, so that it could repair itself. If only Breadbox could have survived. Her return trip to home would soon be ready.

I told Clay about my conversation with Dr. Hu and he said, "Why don't you hire an attorney to enforce your rights in this case?"

On Monday I looked for an attorney that specialized in flying saucer crashes. Hard to find. I called the attorney I've used for copyright infringement issues. I got his voicemail. "Sorry, can't take your call just now. I'm engaged in a virtual wine tasting."

Virtual wine tasting? What the heck was that? Sounded very unsatisfying. Was it something like sexting? Oh, baby, do you get those black cherry notes? Yes! Yes! And the licorice. It lingers on the back of my palate. Now it's coming through. The charcoal!!! Oh-h-h, I can't take it any more. Enough of that.

When he called me back, he dissuaded me. "You know, it will cost you $50,000 just to get into court, and well into six figures to go up against the Feds. That's one of the things they do to prevail, is wear you down financially. Unless it's a case that's likely to go to the Supreme Court. Then you might find a public interest law firm to take up your cause. But somehow I doubt that the issue of who owns a piece of space junk falls into that category."

"This is no ordinary space junk!" I yelled at the phone.

"And all they would have to say is, 'It was actually our experimental vessel that crashed there, so it belongs to us. This woman has no claim.'"

"You mean they would lie?" Hah! "Well, did you see the photos of those alien beings they dug up? How would they account for that? Those are just from their weird breeding experiments, right?"

But I got his point.

That's when Plan B began to take shape.

A couple of days later, Dr. Hu called me again, and invited—begged, pleaded! me to come down to Edwards out in the Mojave to see the reconstructed vessel. He couldn't promise—but he was quite sure—that they would be willing to pay me quite well to return the missing pieces. Whoever "they" were. I was visualizing $24 worth of wampum beads.

But I didn't say no.

I said I wanted to bring my friend Clay with me as a witness and for moral support, but he said, no only me, don't worry, nobody was going to abduct me.

"Are you going to pay for my travel?"

"No, I'm sorry, I have no budget for that." They could spend a truckload of money to haul the thing off my property and off to a secret hideaway, but couldn't spring for my airline ticket.

So I got a cheap flight to Vegas, rented a car, and drove back to Edwards AFB in Mojave.

Only then did I realize that Area 51 of UFO fame is actually part of the same hush-hush flight-test facility, just across the Nevada state line from Edwards. Spooky.

32. Not That Far from Area 51

Scattered o'er all the worlds
Lie untold grains of sand
On every beach, forgotten shore
More grains of sand there are
Than stars in all the cosmos.
Sand grains, there are many more.
From "Agate on the Cosmic Shore" on Inner-Galactic Journey album

There was my spaceship, out of its hangar, on a low flatbed railroad car in the immensity of the Mojave Desert. Thoroughly tied down to the ground like a wild stallion raring to escape. But it didn't look that wild. Like a long, dull, gray tube, about the color of Wanda. One end was slightly pointed, and had a black cap. The other end—the stern? was a bit thicker, and was rounded. At its thickest spot was a large, black band, like a giant rubber O-ring around the vessel's girth. And a dull-gray stripe along the side, kind of like the running board on an old sedan. No wings, no fins, no antennas, no other protuberances, no observation ports.

One round port near the front, maybe five feet in diameter, was propped open, with a stepladder leaned against it. Assorted cables and large light fixtures on tall stands were strewn around, plus many other mysterious instruments, connected by a spaghetti of electric wires. A diesel generator on wheels chugged away nearby, destroying the serenity of the desert.

No rocket tubes. So where's the propulsion? What makes it go? Was that one of the still-missing pieces? But it looked pretty complete. No big gaps left to be filled in. At least not on the outside.

Seeing this unprepossessing thing, you'd never think it had leapt between stars with a cargo of living beings.

Ed said, "Want to take a look inside?" Of course! We climbed up the stepladder, me first, and stepped inside. I was disoriented at first, until I remembered that this was the first time I'd been inside when it wasn't upside down. The crew's harnesses made a lot more sense when viewed from this perspective.

I teared up, despite myself. It brought back such a flood of memories, from the time I first stepped inside here and rescued Breadbox. We had spent so much time inside this tiny metal coffin. So many excellent memories. I wiped my eyes on my sleeve and made sure I kept my face turned away from him.

Ed went to the life-support apparatus and pulled it toward us. "We have figured out how it regenerates its atmosphere to keep it breathable, and how the crew's life support worked. Through tubes that plugged into those holes in their sides that we found on their bodies. Apparently took care of both feeding and elimination."

"You mean they went to the bathroom through the same tube they ate from?" Yuck! But at least that mystery was solved.

"Two parallel tubes within the same housing."

I took a bunch of photos with my phone, even though the uniformed guys at the gate had told me sternly not to, but Ed didn't stop me.

"And look here," he said, like a young boy with a new toy box. "We're quite sure these grids were used to generate an artificial gravity field. But we may have to take it up into zero G to test it. And before it repaired itself, we noticed a complex magnetic metal foam right inside the outer hull that we think protected them from the radiation of outer space. There are some brilliant things here that we can adapt right away for our own space program!"

"How did they fly it?" I asked, puzzled, because I'd never been able to figure this out.

"Down that narrow passageway, that you could probably crawl down easier than me, is the pilot's console. And another nearby for what must have been the navigator." We both crawled through. "But this is where there seem to be some missing pieces. There's a platform with several joystick-looking things that they may have sat on. But it doesn't seem to be enough. Perhaps they gave it commands by thought. Or perhaps it was completely automatic. Or operated remotely by some other entity."

"Hmm. Guided by thought." That is something I had never considered, nor seen any evidence of that between Breadbox and Wanda. "Well, you have to consider all the possibilities."

"It's easy to disassemble and put back together, so we've been able to dig around in the inner workings, up to a point. It reminds me of the old Volkswagen Bug I restored when I was a kid. With a manual, I was able to do all kinds of things with it. No manual here, though."

He pointed to an opening in the nav console—just the size to hold Wanda. "Whatever fit in here may have been important. But that's one of the pieces we haven't found—yet."

Hint, hint. Should I give "it" back to him? Hmm. No way. Not yet, anyway. I'd have to think long and hard about what I'd want from him and his "top men," in order for me to give up my two critical pieces of the puzzle. It wasn't about money. What would I want assurances of, and how could that be guaranteed, once I'd given up my leverage?

"So, Dr. Hu, I really appreciate this tour. You've taken very good care of the spacecraft. My question: When do I get it back?"

This took him completely off guard. His calm demeanor was penetrated, and he actually did a double take. I could see, in his mind, that he'd already taken possession of the pink slip.

He spoke in a high-pitched, pleading voice. "You can't have it back. We've just begun our studies. There's a wealth of technology here that we can learn about to benefit all of humanity."

"Perhaps I would lease it back to you if I were convinced that it would indeed be for the benefit of all humanity, rather than just an exclusive cadre of American scientists and government officials. And generals.

"We scientists have an exemplary record of sharing our discoveries among all nationalities. Perhaps you think it should be turned over to the United Nations."

"Is that the same United Nations that is dominated by some of the most thuggish, people-denying regimes in the world?"

"Well, I don't think the UN is that bad."

"Faint praise. You haven't answered my question."

"Where would you keep it? Back in your field? As a valuable asset, the IRS would have it appraised, and then tax you based on its assessed value."

"Hah! That's just what I would expect! Send in the IRS to do your dirty work! But how would they appraise it? There's not much of a market on used flying saucers to get comparables."

"As you well know, this vessel is worth a fortune. You'd be taxed on what it would be worth. They do that all the time."

"If it was worth that much, then I could sell it and afford to pay the taxes. Or perhaps just sell the rights to study it."

"So this IS about money!"

"Not really. Look, I don't want my epitaph to say, 'She died filthy rich but unleashed a firestorm of violent competition on the world for these alien technologies.'"

"That's a long epitaph, but I get your meaning. And I completely agree with you that we want to keep that from happening."

"Maybe we should haul it farther out in the desert and detonate a small nuke inside it."

He nodded his head. "Yeah, that thought has occurred to me, and to others. But you know, there's no way we would ever do that. I believe that destroying this knowledge—this window into the Universe—would be as big a crime, and sin, as allowing a violent confrontation over it."

"I agree. First of all, it would be like murdering a sentient being." He looked at me thoughtfully, as if seriously considering that the vessel was alive. Who was I to deny this?

Changing tenor, I asserted loudly," I am not relinquishing my claim to this clever beast!" Then softening, I followed with, "And by the way, when will it be ready to take us for a spin out around Mars?"

"As soon as you return the missing piece," he said, with his knowing grin.

As I turned away to leave, I couldn't help but smile. I hadn't had this much fun in a long time.

I had no idea what I was going to do.

When I got back up to my real world on the Sonoma coast, I found I had an invitation to do another gig at Locos Only. Maybe I'd dream up another stanza to "Space Girl Yearning" before then.

I did dream that night, about flying Breadbox and her crew in the refurbished vessel, with Wanda restored to her proper receptacle, back to their home world. I steered the vessel in expertly over a mauve sea and landed amidst yellow trees. Then strange beings with ominous weapons came and arrested me as I emerged. I woke up sweating and trembling and sobbing. I ran out onto the front deck without putting on a stitch of clothing, and screamed and howled at the full moon about to set into the ocean. Good thing I have no close neighbors.

Not long afterward, my buddies threw me a party on the one-year anniversary of The Crash. We barbequed steak and chicken on my deck, and grilled corn and peppers. Clay brought some wonderful Malbec.

"This evening is so much like the one a year ago," he said as he poured, "when we were sitting here, chairs arranged in exactly the same way."

"Yeah, we're all in the same spots," I agreed. "It's our ritual, isn't it?"

"I'm praying for no more sonic booms just now," said Jim, and everybody nodded.

We watched the sun sink into the cloudbank on the horizon, and deep into the dusk, we recounted the crash and our memories of Breadbox.

Sheriff Jim quickly got tired of our apologies to him. He was taking his suspension stoically. "This is on me. I can't blame you folks. Besides, it's unclear what the problem is. Seems like political hysteria. Despite what you've heard, this is paid leave. And I'm getting lots of stuff done around the place. It's my poor wife having to put up with me that you should feel sorry for." Meg did a Mona Lisa smile and gave his hand a squeeze.

I told them about my visit to Edwards, how the vessel was repairing itself, and what I had learned from Wanda.

Clay asked, "Are you ever going to get it back?"

"No way!" Doc responded, "They'll never give up control!"

"I'm not giving up on it. I'm not sure what I'm going to do, but it's my spaceship."

Clay looked unconvinced, but played along, "If you're going to have a vessel, you have to name it. What should you call it?"

"Hmm, I hadn't thought of that yet. But you're right. Suggestions?"

"What about Icarus!" shouted Meg. "Rising from Earth toward the stars!"

"Oh, and crashing and burning," retorted Clay.

"Yeah, it has already crashed once," I frowned. "Hope it got that out of its system."

"How can something fall from space and not blast itself to smithereens?" asked Doc.

"It didn't crash from space. Basically, it just made a terribly bad landing," I said, defensively.

"What about Niña?" Meg persisted. "You know, Pinta, Niña, and Santa Maria? Columbus's ships of discovering the New World?"

"Ooh I like that!" said Jim, joining the conversation.

"Maybe I should name it Breadbox," I said. "Or use her real name."

Clay asked, "Doesn't it already have a name?'

"Ah! Maybe so! But Breadbox never referred to her ship in a personal way."

Later I asked Wanda the Wand what the name of the vessel was. Maybe it had some romantic name. But no, it just had a number. They hadn't given it a special name.

I needed a name that would relate to Breadbox and her friends. I decided to name it "*Star Choice*."

Now that it had a name, should I stencil it on the bow? To do that, I'd have to sneak back into its near-Area 51 hideaway.

33. Space Girl Yearning

My Locos Only gig that Saturday was one of my best ever. I ended up doing two complete sets. I was totally hoarse by the end, well after midnight. The place was jammed and overflowing both times. I let it all hang out. I made up a couple of songs right on the spot, about my reluctance to sing my own truth. I came as close as I ever have to divulging that I'd nurtured an alien in my backyard, and how I had learned so much from her. Paparazzi and stupid tabloid stories be damned. It's time for me to be telling the truth about things. Especially about myself.

Later that night back at home, after turning off all the lights, drawing the blinds, and watching for lurking spies (perhaps named Doctor Who), I got Wanda out from beneath the floorboard, put her on my bed, and asked her a few questions.

"Wanda, how does the vessel get its fuel to power itself?"

"It is already in the power module." Hmm, that must be pretty compact and powerful fuel, and not be recognizable as fuel by the engineers there.

"Can you talk to it?"

"Yes, Wanda communicates with it continually."

"Do you guide its self-repairs?"

"Yes, and it is much easier now that they have placed it near large metal objects from which it can draw molecules and crystals of the materials it needs." I imagined the derelict aircraft being gradually weakened by having their molecules of metal sucked out until they collapsed in a heap.

"Can you ask it to fly to us?"

"Yes Wanda can do that, once the repairs are complete."

"Could you return to the home world of Breadbox?"

"Wanda is capable of doing that. Wanda would do that only if you requested it to do so."

"Can you again connect me with her home clan?"

"Wanda is no longer able to do that. They have severed the connection, since they requested that Wanda self-destruct."

"Oh, that's terrible! Does that mean we can never again connect with the devices of your Confederation?"

"Wanda can connect you with any other device on the Confederation network on any other world throughout our stellar systems. Wanda can access data wells there as long as our credential number is retained."

Fascinating. From my coastside aerie, here on a remote world in a corner of the galaxy, I can tap into the information reserves of the Universe! Google, eat your heart out!

"So we could travel to other stars in the Confederation."

"To the worlds of those stellar systems, yes. But complications may arise."

"What kind of complications?"

"You may not be welcome. It would be best to work out arrangements before travel."

"Yes, I always do that."

A long pause to get up my nerve for the next question. "So if I so choose, and I made suitable arrangements, I could travel with you and the vessel to other worlds."

"Yes."

"And come back?"

"In principle. Complications can arise. Wanda would be dedicated to protecting you."

"Yet your former crew crashed and failed to survive. You did not protect them."

"They neglected to follow Wanda's instructions upon approaching this world."

Oh yeah, there's that. And I've always been so good at following directions.

Then Wanda pointed out to me that I don't have to physically explore. Through her, and using robot probes like those Novan had crafted, the plans of which she contained within her, I could explore the Confederation from my rocking chair.

Hmmm. Why did that suggestion leave me so flat?

*   *   *

There you have it. I had the power. I alone had the power, to command a space vessel capable of traveling to worlds all over this corner of space. What an adventure that would be!

I went out on my deck despite the chill and just drank in the universe— the infinite riot of stars above. My thoughts were whizzing back and forth. I was elated, thrilled, excited! I was dancing up and down and running around and whooping.

Did I dare do this?

I was terrified! It's foolish to even think of doing this. It would end in disaster. A suicide mission. Who the hell did I think I was, even thinking about setting off across the cosmos alone with a smart-ass talking tube? Cooped up in a tin can for who knows how long? I couldn't survive by sticking a feeding tube in my side.

No, I could do it. Breadbox said the trip was quite fast. This is not the Voyager mission taking decades to get out of the solar system. I'd be well-received. We'd sing to each other on new worlds. I'd return with a lifetime of song material.

Don't be ridiculous! I wouldn't be able to breathe the air or eat the food. I'd die of a horrible disease. My shivering wasn't just from the cold.

No, not so. I'd have Wanda to watch over me. We wouldn't go where we weren't welcome.

Right, like she watched over Breadbox and crew. Time to put this crazy idea out of your mind.

But it wouldn't stay down. I kept musing.

I'd be the ambassador from Earth to the Galactic Confederation. They'd welcome us as valued members.

If Earth was going to send an ambassador, it sure wouldn't be some ditzy California musician with a checkered past.

More likely, I'd alert the Galactics to the existence of an upstart planet on their periphery, and they'd follow me back to keep us in our place.

But still. Hmmm.

This mind-forking could go on forever. Let me think on it.

I'd had a good life as a singer and a composer. I'd had my share of fame and fortune. My singing could easily carry me through the rest of my life. I'd be quite comfortable, and have some renown. I had good friends, who'd stuck with me through this episode, at some cost to themselves.

On the other hand, I could explore the stars. I could be a space girl! I had a star-leaping vessel, and an omnipotent guide in Wanda. First Earth woman to the Galactic Confederation! I could become the stuff of myths. And have one hell of a good time!

"I don't know what I'll do," I said to nobody as I went back inside. "But I don't have to decide now. Not until the repairs are finished. Just knowing I have the power might be enough."

I felt a song coming on—a new verse to Space Girl Yearning. Oh, I had that space girl yearning!

> *Space girl yearn–ing*
> *De–sire burn–ing*
> *Pull–ing me away*
> *From all who love me*
> *From all my duty*
> *Just to soar away*
> > *How will I ever find my way*
> > *Will I ever return one day*
> > *And will they still love me if I do?*
> *Song girl yearning*
> *Big bucks earning*
> *Heart song spurning*
> *Pulling me away*
> *From all who love me*

From all my beauty
It's just another day.
> *When will I ever sing my song*
> *Will my fan girls sing along*
> *And will they still pay me if I do?*
Space girls cry–ing
Slow–ly dy–ing
How can we turn the day?
Can we ever turn the day?

34. My Spaceship Calls Out to Me

My spaceship calls out to me
Come fly me home
I'm yours, you're my skipper.
Just call and I'll come.
      From Inner-Galactic Journey album

At 3:15 am, a couple of months later, my phone rang. "Dr. Hu! What prompts you to call at this hour?" I sat up straight on the edge of my bed with Wanda at my side.

"You know damn well! I was awakened at three by the sound of cables popping. I ran outside just in time to see our friend rising straight up without a sound."

"I didn't know you slept beside it."

"You are operating it remotely. Did you send it home?"

Star Choice escapes from the Mojave

I remained silent. Did I really want to tell him my part in this? I couldn't hold it in.

"No, I didn't send it home. I asked it to orbit around the Moon for now. You can probably see it with a decent telescope."

"You asked it? How exactly did you do that?"

"Ed, can I call you Ed?"

"Call me an idiot, for letting you get away when I had you here!"

"Ed, I had to retrieve my property. You weren't going to give it back to me."

"You're crazy, woman! What are you going to do with it?" He sounded like a little boy who'd lost his toy.

"Leverage, for one thing. Now it's under my control, so we can talk sense about certain things. There are many things you want that I would love to give you. But there are a few things I want in return."

"Like what?"

"I don't want to get into the whole thing at 3:30 a.m. Except for one thing: Sheriff Jim Osborne must be fully reinstated, with back pay and no adverse marks on his dossier."

"Hah! Impossible. That's completely out of my hands."

"I doubt that. See what you can do. Then let's talk again." I hung up.

He called back the next afternoon. "I think all is well with your good sheriff." Great! He did the impossible in twelve hours! Good man to know.

"I am so grateful to you for helping with that," I admitted. I felt I had to give him something. "Ed, there's something I haven't told you."

"Oh yeah, only one thing?" Sounded a bit truculent, wouldn't you say?

"There was a third crewmember, who lived for a while, then died. She told me a lot about where she came from, how they got here, how they live, why she came, and so on."

"Oh yeah? How was her English?" Dripping with sarcasm, but I'm used to that.

"Not so good. But we taught each other some language, and there was a language translator."

"Evidence for this preposterous claim?"

"My evidence is currently in orbit around the Moon."

"Point taken. We have actually spotted it. It travels very rapidly! Many times faster than any of our Moon shots." More heavy breathing. He kept drawing in a breath as if he was about to say something, but then didn't. Finally, "Okay, first, I want to take back all the times I've called you a ditzy chick. Clearly not true. You are a worthy adversary." I could tell it hurt him to blurt these words out.

"Why, thank you. But we need to become allies, not adversaries. And of course that will work better if you don't view me as a ditzy chick. Dr. Hu—Ed—I owe you a huge debt of gratitude. I could not have done this without your help. If you and your people hadn't dredged up and reassembled all the pieces, so that the spaceship could repair itself, it would still be a pile of junk. You would learn valuable lessons from it, but it could never again have flown."

Grumble, humph. "Well, I'm dying to know how you are communicating with the vessel."

"Telepathy," I hedged, not yet wanting to give him any ideas about Wanda. "Her name is *Star Choice*, FYI. Where do I register the name for a spaceship? FAA or NASA?"

"*Star Choice*, eh? Is that your choice?"

"Going to the stars was the choice of those who came here." I teared up remembering this. I whispered to myself, "This is for you, Breadbox, my best friend."

"Ed, I have a lot of exciting things to share with you. I have no idea what I want to do next. It's time I tell you the whole story. It could take awhile."

"I'm all ears."

"Your tardis awaits, Doctor Who. I'm thinking of putting together a crew. Astrophysics would be a useful skill. Is there anybody you'd recommend?"

Hee hee! This is the best time I've ever had!

Epilogue - A Glimpse Forward
to Book 2, My Spaceship Calls Out to Me

Star Choice landed shortly before dawn under Wanda's guidance, right near where I was standing. The sliver of moon in the east gave scant illumination. Three stubby landing supports extended at the last moment, and the hundred-ton vessel landed as light as a dirigible, silent except for the crunch of lava gravel. The port opened with a sigh, the step folded down, and soft light poured out. I turned and waved at Mike, hoping he could see me against the open port. Yes! He flashed his headlights. Could be my last greeting with a fellow human.

I turned and stepped inside—as easy as getting on the bus. The air inside was sweeter, moister, and a bit higher pressure than the dry mountain air.

The port closed with a satisfyingly soft but solid sound, and my ears popped slightly. Light emanating from the wall panels was just strong enough for me to find my way to the captain's seat. Before I sat, I looked around, enthralled.

Only then did it hit me. I was slammed by a flood of emotions that took my breath away. Like coming out on stage at my first big concert in the Hollywood Bowl with the dazzling lights and the crowd wildly cheering. I was ecstatic and terrified! All our dreams and discussions and sketches had come to life inside this beautiful spaceship—including the two empty seats meant for my missing Spaceketeers, alas. I burst out crying from sadness and aloneness. I was about to fly off to the Moon by myself in an untested vessel. My knees wobbled from terror. I turned toward the now-closed port. Was it too late too get out and cancel the trip?

"Get ahold of yourself, woman!" I yelled the way Clay would do. I took a deep breath, then another. Inhale, exhale. Phew. Got my heart rate back down to jackhammer mode.

Okay, back to business. I stowed my gear in an enclosure back near my bed, noting the cartons of uninstalled fixtures in the rear.

I settled into my custom-outfitted space seat and closed the restraints across my lap and chest. The view space popped into existence right in front of me, and Wanda's soft voice emanated from it. "Welcome to *Star Choice*, my controlling oki."

I could now see everything in front of the vessel in 3-D, as if I was looking through a large porthole window. Better actually, because the view space accentuated the light.

"All systems are functioning properly," Wanda announced with what to me sounded like a touch of pride, "and we are ready to depart as soon as you request."

"Let's go to the Moon, Wanda!" I shouted, and instantly felt a slight push back into my seat. The antigravity—or grav—canceled most of the feeling of acceleration, because we leapt off the ground as if shot out of a cannon. By the time I looked, we were already ten thousand feet above the ground, according to the view space readout and my view of Mauna Kea receding. The rate of acceleration was unbelievable; in a few seconds the Sun burst over the black horizon like a skyrocket, and then its brilliance was surrounded by the blackness of space and a riot of stars.

I was merely a passenger. I had discussed our flight plan with Wanda, my magical metallic companion, and now she was at the helm, even though she was safely ensconced back in California. When I had placed the remote—the piece she had created for me that Clay had taken to Tinian with him—into the receptacle meant for her in the instrument console, she became the brains for the space ship. Or perhaps better to say, it became her body.

Even with the grav limiting the G-force of acceleration, I felt the irresistible push down into my seat. It signified the vast power at my command. I could hear unsecured cartons of fixtures sliding across the floor toward the rear.

The acceleration continued. We were moving so rapidly that I could see the arc of the Moon increase in size and move against the background of stars as we raced toward it. I asked Wanda to show the aft view, and saw the blue and green and white Earth receding.

Seeing the Earth, it hit me again. The most amazing feeling I've ever had in my life. My tears were flowing so hard I could barely see. I started singing, to keep from crying. Also Sprach Zarathustra from 2001 Space Odyssey. I yelled it out full voice, waving my arms to conduct the imaginary orchestra.

There was California off to the left side, on the leading edge of the continent, just coming into daylight. "Wanda, can we see my house?" The view space zoomed in, making my stomach feel like it does during the Big Drop on the roller coaster.

"This is the maximum," Wanda informed me. I could clearly see Bodega Bay and the Farallones, as well as the Golden Gate, but I could not make out my house through the morning fog. Then we were past it.

"Wanda, let's see Andromeda." The view faded, then re-emerged with Andromeda galaxy spread across the screen in all its glory. Here at last was something so distant it wasn't changing in size as I watched it. It was so large! What before I had seen in the sky as Andromeda was only the bright central core. Against the blackness of space, its feathery arms spread out eight to ten times farther.

"Wanda, can we spot the home world of Breadbox?" The viewscreen zoomed in on a dark portion of the sky, as stars moved out of the field of vision. The view kept boring into the darkness, moving past myriad unnamed stars, until, at the limit of magnification, just one speck remained in the center. A small yellow dot, the same color as the Sun. I strained in vain to spot a tiny blue-green world nearby. "Breadbox, my best friend, this trip is for you." I burst into tears all over again thinking of my departed friend in whose vessel I was flying.

Back to the Moon view. Wow, I could feel that we were already decelerating! Since we were coming in on the dark side, the Moon went from sliver of light to black disk against the stars, and then eclipsed the Sun. In a moment the Sun emerged on the other side, and then I turned the viewscreen toward the Moon's surface, rushing toward us. In less than a minute, a chime sounded and Wanda informed me that we were in an elliptical orbit around the Moon that would take us quite near the surface. Less than two hours for the entire trip!

I was orbiting the Moon! I was orbiting the Moon! On my very first foray into space. I wanted to tell all my friends. No, I wanted my friends to be here. All of them. This wasn't supposed to be a one-woman trip!

"Wanda, can we call up my Spaceketeers? And Doc and Clay? And Jonn and Noel? And what's for breakfast?"

I sang out the refrain from my just-recorded song, with Wanda humming harmony, just as she had during the last jam session with Breadbox:

> *Just call and I'll come to you*
> *And we'll fly away soon.*
> *Across the wide heavens*
> *Far past the Moon*
>
> *Just call and I'll come to you*
> *The whole galaxy's our home*
> *On any world anywhere*
> *Just call and I'll come.*

"Hee hee!"

Extras for My Readers

Characters and Names in Aliens Crashed In My Back Yard

Selena M. The protagonist who is narrating the story. She's a singer/songwriter who was growing bored with her music and thought she might be going over the hill. Her real name is Berthe Morisot Monahan. "That's Bear-tuh, not Birth-a," she insists.

Breadbox. Nickname of a very non-human alien survivor of spaceship crash on the hill behind Selena's house on the coast near Bodega Bay, north of San Francisco. Selena discovered her in the crash, and decided to nurse her back to health instead of turning her (and the crashed vessel) over to the authorities. They learn to communicate by singing. Her real name is Bvar-nala-nga. Nala for short.

Agate. Nickname given by Breadbox to Selena. Beautiful gem among all the grains of sand on the cosmic shore.

Clay, Jim and **Meg Osborne, Doc.** Neighbors and friends of Selena. Jim is the local sheriff; his wife Meg is kind of square; Doc is a veterinarian and belongs to a survivalist organization. Clay is a high school teacher and has a crush on Selena.

Wanda. The "personal multi-function device" that belonged to Breadbox. Selena said it looked like a magic wand, and called it Wanda the Wand. It was a foot-long metallic cylinder, but came to adopt a personality at the urging of Selena, who called it a "she."

Morty. The musician's agent of Selena. Excitable New Yorker, always urging Selena to take music gigs.

Eddy Backwater. Country singer who is ill-mannered and sneaky and gives Selena fits.

Dr. Hu. Edwin X. Hu, PhD, is an astrophysicist employed by the government to retrieve missing pieces of the spaceship from Selena.

Dana. Teaching assistant of Professor Bunker. He disbelieves Selena's story, but Dana wants it to be true.

Star Choice. Name that Selena gives to the crashed spaceship once it is repaired and ready to fly.

Sfofong. Name of Breadbox's home world. Her people are the Fofonoloy.

Alala and **Novan**. The two crew members of Breadbox who died in the crash. Their complete names were Analala-noa, female, the inventor and researcher and captain; and Rleza-novan-nga, male, engineer and navigator.

Kateh. Clan mother of Breadbox on Sfofong.

oki. A term for any intelligent, technology-using being or race. From Fedi, the language of the Confederation. There's a lot of argument about just who is considered to be oki, but that's a whole different story.

Clubs Where Selena Performs

These don't actually exist, but they should.

Locos Only. The local dive down in the flats in Bodega Bay, near where Selena lives.

Berzerkly. Night club near UC Berkeley. Hip clientele.

Club Xanadu. In Venice CA, near the beach in the Los Angeles area. Attracts many tourists, because it's named after the club in the movie Xanadu starring Olivia Newton John.

Slick Slim's Slither Inn. In Venice, almost next door to Club Xanadu. Attracts a raucous, down and dirty crowd.

The Bowl. Point Arena, CA. A natural amphitheatre in this small coastal town in Northern California.

Explanation of Alien Science: How to Jump Between Stars
(from Chapter 20)

"You are saying that you and your crew traveled from your world to ours—a distance that it takes light about 4,000 of our years to travel—in a very short time?"

"But of course we used the star jump. We didn't actually travel all that distance."

"Wait. I don't understand this," I interrupted. "How does this work? What does it mean to 'jump' between worlds? Our science tells us this is impossible."

Here's how I pieced it together.

The universe has two (or more?) kinds of space, overlaid. Regular space has all the laws and limits we are familiar with. The other space has different laws. Laws that allow messages, solid things, and even living beings to move from one place to another without passing through the intervening space. Space without distance. Perhaps without time.

It's like on Earth. We can travel on foot only so fast and so far. But suppose there's a telephone where I'm heading. I can just call ahead, seemingly instantaneous. "Telephone space" is completely different from travel-by-foot space. A telephone seems like magic to someone who has never encountered one before. But once you get used to it, you never again send messages by runner.

But initially there are no phones. So somebody first has to travel around on foot to install phones at different locations. They assign each one a number, record it in a directory along with its location, and thereafter you can reach that location merely by calling the number. Now, when you call a phone number, you may have no idea where that phone is located, and maybe you don't care. You only want to connect with the person on the other end.

In a broad swath of our galaxy, probably millions of years ago, robot vessels chugged around between stars at sub-light speed, taking as long as it took, installing jumpsites around stars with interesting planets, like a fleet of cosmic Johnny Appleseeds. Jumpsites were positioned at stable gravitational spots, where they would stay put over eons in relation to the worlds they wanted to visit. Thereafter, vessels could get there by jumping through the other plane of space —the one with no time or distance—from one star to another.

Unlike the "telephone space" network, with this "space jumpsite" network, you could send not only messages, but also vessels and people and goods.

But in the intervening millions of years the "phone directory" of jumpsites had been lost. Not just the directory, but also the knowledge of those who had created the network and its directory. And even the system of recording the data was lost! Later, when bits of it were found, people didn't recognize it for what it was. Yet the jumpsites themselves still orbited their stars, awaiting a visitor.

Much more recently (tens of thousands of years?), the existing Confederation built up a new network of jumpsites as it expanded. It wasn't as extensive as the prior network; old jumpsites at stars like our Sun lay completely outside the newer network. Also, it was based on a completely different system of communication.

I can't quite grasp the distinction, but it sounds like the more recent Confederation used strings of numbers to identify jumpsites—the way we would do it—whereas the ancient prior civilization had used complex pieces of song. You can see how singing storytellers like the Fofonoloy would be the ones to rediscover them.

The Four Body Types of Confederation World Races
(from Chapter 9)

Breadbox was silent for some time. "Another factor. Peoples of our body shape are less welcome. Most oki world races look more like people from your world—standing upright with four or six fixed appendages. These are Type 1 bodies, which evolved on solid surfaces. The Fofonoloy evolved on a wet world, in swamps and marshes. We have Type 2 bodies, with varying numbers of appendages, and without a solid skeleton."

"How many body types are there?" I asked.

"Four types on oxygen worlds. Type 3 beings live in the deep sea, and have appendages specialized for water. Type 4 live on dry land. They lack internal skeletons, but have an external hard structure.

"Type 4 sounds like bugs! I'm sorry to interrupt."

"I treasure your questions. What is a 'bugs?'"

"Bug. We see them all around us. That one is called a spider, this one buzzing around us is a fly. That blue one flying rapidly is called a dragonfly. Some fly, some crawl. Six or eight legs.

"I see. On your world Type 4 is called 'bugs.' Our Type 4 races that are oki are larger. But they have trouble communicating with Type 1 oki."

"Why were your Type 2 people the Fofonoloy less welcome on other worlds?"

"Because we are different from most oki races. They are suspicious of us. We also communicate in a unique manner, mostly by singing. And we cannot eat the same food as others. Only Type 4 oki are viewed with more suspicion and hostility.

Song Lyrics

Lyrics marked with an asterisk have been recorded and appear on **galaxytalltales.com.**

*My Space Ship Calls Out to Me
My space ship calls out to me
Come fly me home
I'm yours, you're my skipper.
Just call and I'll come.

Just call and I'll come to you
And we'll fly away soon.
Across the wide heavens
Far past the Moon

Just call and I'll come to you
We'll build up a crew
To explore all the heavens
But I'll heed only you.

Just call and I'll come to you
Leave the king in the dust
We'll explore the wide heavens.
With just those you trust."

Just call and I'll come to you
The whole galaxy's our home
On any world anywhere
Just call and I'll come.

Spacegirls Yearning
Spacegirl yearn-ing
De-sire burn-ing
Pull-ing me away
From all who love me
From all my duty
Just to soar away
      How will I ever find my way
      Will I ever return one day
      And will they still love me if I do?

Song girl yearning
Big bucks earning
Heart song spurning
Pulling me away
From all who love me
From all my beauty
It's just another day.
> When will I ever sing my song
> Will my fan girls sing along
> And will they still pay me if I do?

Spacegirls cry-ing
Slow-ly dy-ing
How can we turn the day?
Can we ever turn the day?

*Cotton Candy Lovin'

Cotton candy lovin', that's all I seem to find
It makes you high, that sugar lovin' kind.
But soon I crash, I hit the floor
It leaves me hungry, wantin' more

Spun like sugar
whipped up dreams
Cotton candy lovin'
ain't what it seems

It don't fill your belly
It can't fill your soul

Broken promises
Shattered dreams
Cotton candy lovin'
ain't what it seems.

I search again, to see who I can find.
Just another sugar lovin' kind.
That's cotton candy love, but I don't mind.

Anthem to My Secret Self

I've been a sweet stuff singer
All my girlie years
Airy, frothy little ditties

Full of love and tears
If the world only knew me
And knew what I could do
If the world could only see me
And appreciate the view
       No scoffing, "She's just a girl."

Inside I'm a hero
I often save the world
I smite the bad guys, save the good
Pretty good for just a girl!
       Thank you, Super Girl!

My inner self's a beauty
When will I show the world?
But I'm afraid you'll brush me off
Or ignore me, even worse.
       Scoffing, "She's just a girl."

I honor myself; it's time to shine
To do what I can do
To tell my truth, to claim what's mine
To sing my inner song to you
And sing my inner song
       The song of Super Girl.

Anthem of the Alien—sung by Breadbox

The universe is cold and uncaring
life is a nothingful scum.

We life, we call ourselves smart ones;
we use our brave tools
to guide our smart pebbles
from sun to sun to sun.

We build temples and towers,
our passions and stories,
our shames, our wars,
our conquests and glories
while starwheels spin uncaring above.

We life, we always crave meaning
where no meaning can ever be found.
So let us create some meaning
just to keep ourselves happy and found
and to build our short lives around

Thus we sing and continue the story
the most valuable gem that we hold.
Tell our fleeting hope and our glory.
If song dies, so too dies our meaning
so sing it till heavens grow cold.

Reprise

So, let us light a spark
and share it now together
I ask you: come share my light
my warmth and song
Let's tell tall tales, sip a warm mug,
and laugh the whole night long
In the morn sun, a hug,
a cup of brew
to rekindle our warmth
in the cool of early dew.

Benediction: Accept my ode to our friendship and our joy of singing together.

Response by Selena M

'Cross all the worlds, across all space
The song of love has but one face.
I see your face, I see your love
I hear your voice, I hear your song
The sacred song of everywhere
With thee this night I share.

May those on all the worlds we know
And others that lie beyond
Pick up our hymn, our sacred song
And know that they are part of it
And know that we are one.

Amen.

Mike Van Horn

I started writing science fiction thirty years ago, but other writing to make a living got in the way. Lots of non-fiction how-to books aimed at small business owners. Two books published plus over a dozen self-published, all built around our consulting business, The Business Group.

Then my wife and I went to a workshop called Unfinished Business. I saw that if I was ever going to get my stories done in this lifetime I'd better get going! Since then I have concentrated on writing sci fi. Aliens Crashed started out as a short story, but metastasized into a trilogy.

My wife BJ is also writing a story about a 19th century English barrister who tangles with the ghost of a beautiful French woman who was wronged. And our daughter Rebecca is a writer also. The whole family is word-crazy!

My non-fiction books include:
– **Understanding Expert Systems** (1985)
– *Pacific Rim Trade* (1989)
– *How to Grow Your Business without Driving Yourself Crazy* (2002)

I have an MBA from University of California, Los Angeles. I still do consulting work, but my sci fi storytelling is a lot more fun.

www.galaxytalltales.com

Writer at work. Haleiwa, Oahu, Hawaii

Want to Read More?

You've just finished Book 1 of a trilogy. Here are the next two: www.galaxytalltales.com

My Spaceship Calls Out to Me

"If I have a spaceship, I might as well fly off to the stars!" says Selena. "You're crazy!" say her friends. "That alien UFO belongs to us, and we're coming to get it!" says the government.

How does she square traipsing into space if she's recommitted to her singing career? And how does she think she can travel in a vessel outfitted for very nonhuman aliens?

The poor spaceship is tied down on the Moon while three government space agencies vie to capture it—or destroy it.

Space Girl Yearning

Selena eludes the government forces just long enough to get into space, but they're still after her—with better weapons. No way can she return to Earth without being captured and losing the spaceship.

And now the aliens from the Confederation of Oxygen Breathing Races are getting involved again. The Galactic Librarian entices her to come sing at the sacred Songstone. Could it be a trap?

But she really wants to go.

Check these out at galaxytalltales.com

. . . plus short stories, like *How I Ended Up with Two Wives* and *Return of the Ancient Ghosts*.

And keep up to date on the next series, *Bleeding Edge*.

www.ingramcontent.com/pod-product-compliance
Lightning Source LLC
Chambersburg PA
CBHW070320120726
47909CB00008B/2522